Lock Down Publications and Ca$h
Presents

I0666787

REDEMPTION IN THE STREETS

Written By
TONY DANIELS

First Edition 2025

Printed in the United States of America

This is a work of fiction. Names, characters, places, and incidents either are products of the author's imagination or are used fictitiously. Any similarity to actual events or locales or persons, living or dead, is entirely coincidental.

Lock Down Publications
P.O. Box 944
Stockbridge, GA 30281
www.lockdownpublications.com

Like our page on Facebook: Lock Down Publications
www.facebook.com/lockdownpublications.ldp

Stay Connected with Us!

Text **LOCKDOWN** to 22828 to stay up-to-date with new releases, sneak peaks, contests and more…

Like our page on Facebook:
Lock Down Publications

Join Lock Down Publications/The New Era Reading Group

Visit our website:
www.lockdownpublications.com

Follow us on Instagram:
Lock Down Publications

Email Us: We want to hear from you!

Acknowledgements

First and foremost, I want to give all praise and thanks to Allah. I want to thank Angelica Daniels for being there when others turned their back on me. You made a great investment in loving me. I will love you forever.

A special shot out to all my family, friends, and fans. I love you all. Follow me on Instagram for more books to come soon: tonydanielstheauthor@yahoo.com

Dedication

To all my fans that been down with me since day one when I first dropped my book Consequence of the Game, you the reason I continued to drop book after book. My passion for writing is real. Thanks to everyone that grabbed a copy of my books and I can inspire you to grab many more with enjoyment.

Chapter 1

Keshia was leaving the beauty shop after collecting her money from the dope girls that owed her. As she walked through the parking lot, she noticed a Honda creeping through slowly. She immediately secured her duffle bag and reached for her 9mm handgun on her hip.

"I don't know who this is, but we can handle this shit right now," Keshia said.

The back window rolled down, and shots rang out. Keshia exchanged gunfire and took cover behind a small car. Bullets flew, shattering the windows. Glass rained down on her. Whoever it was wanted Keshia dead on the spot, and they weren't letting up.

Keshia rose to her feet and let off several shots—then she was hit three times.

"Fuck! Damn!" Keshia screamed in pain.

She dropped to her knees, hitting the pavement from the impact of the bullets. She had been shot in the chest, leg, and shoulder. Lying on the ground, she caught a glimpse of the car's license plate as they sped off. Gritting her teeth, Keshia grabbed her handgun off the ground and fired seven shots, shattering the back window of the car.

Keshia's Benz truck was only a few feet away, but she knew she needed to move quickly because a few people in the hood were watching her and asking if she was okay. She even heard someone yell for the police.

Keshia climbed into her Benz and sped off. Once she was a safe distance away, she peeled off her pink sweatshirt and tossed it in the backseat. Looking down at the bullet holes in her vest, she laughed—the other bullets had only grazed her. She had thought she was hurt badly at the scene of the shooting. Keshia dug into her pocket for her phone and called Nene. After three rings, Nene picked up.

"Hello," Nene answered the phone.

"Hey, friend. I need your help," Keshia said.

"What's wrong, Keshia?" Nene asked.

"Bitch, I'm on my way home on the Northside," Keshia said.

"I'll be there in thirty minutes," Nene said.

Ten minutes later, Keshia pulled up at her crib on the Northside. She jumped out of the car and ran toward her house to open the front door. Once inside, she ripped off her vest and walked to the bathroom.

She turned on the faucet and ran water over her wounds on her body, gritting her teeth as the burning sensation shot through her body. But she had the medical tools to patch up her wounds.

While Keshia was dealing with her wounds, her phone started ringing in her pocket. She reached down, grabbed it, and answered.

"Hello."

"Do you know two young people by the name Coca and Eve?" John asked.

"That's their street name, John." Keshia said, surprised that John didn't greet her first.

"Somebody called in on the hotline dropped some important information saying they're big-time drug dealers out here in the streets," John said.

"Oh yeah? Where you hear that at?" Keshia asked.

"The caller never mentioned your name or Rambo's in this matter?" John said.

Click!

John put on his shoes, ready to head out the front door, but before he could leave, his phone rang. "Hello," John answered.

"I'm cool. You don't have to come over at this moment," Keshia said.

"Okay. My friend over here anyways, and we have some business to handle," John said. He walked back into the house, where Mimi was standing naked in the front room. Mimi stepped closer and started undressing John slowly.

"Don't say a damn word," Mimi whispered. "Just let me handle this."

John didn't say a word. He just watched Mimi do her thang.

Once John was totally undressed, Mimi laid him on the large couch, but he jumped back up and ran into the bedroom. Mimi followed close behind.

"The other night, you showed a bitch everything. Now tonight, John, I want to show you what I've learned," Mimi said as she began kissing his bare chest.

"I'm new at this, so don't get mad if a bitch mess up," she added, easing her tongue towards his rock-hard dick.

"No biting, right?" she asked.

Grabbing John's dick with her small hand, she began licking around its tender and sensitive head. Then, she gently grabbed both his nuts with her other hand and slowly massaged each of them as she continued to lick around the head of his dick.

As John laid quiet with both eyes closed, Mimi took him deep in her throat. As she went up and down with a slow motion, John couldn't control the orgasm that was fast approaching.

"Come here, baby! I'm about to cum in your mouth," John said.

"Not yet, I'm not ready," Mimi said as she continued to massage his nuts and sucked every bit of him like a movie porn star.

"Ah, shit!" John yelled out as he uncontrollably bust off. Without a pause, Mimi calmly held onto his dick and swallowed every single drop, making sure nothing was wasted.

"Did I handle that dick right?" Mimi asked.

"Nice," John said, shaking his head in disbelief.

His mind drifted to Keshia. She had called needing his help, but after he mentioned Coca and Eve, she changed her mind.

"Okay, I'll let you rest for a few minutes. Then it's time for round two," Mimi said.

"What have I created over these past years with you, Mimi?" John asked.

"A big monster, that's what you created. You common-law married to me now," Mimi said, laying on John's chest. "All you have to do is take care of your business in bed. Are you my husband or not?"

Mimi laughed, slapping John's chest playfully. For the rest of the night, Mimi took John's mind away from being a law enforcement officer at that moment, making sure he only focused on her.

"Mimi, you love sucking this dick?" John asked.

"A white husband like you ain't never had a black woman sucking your dick this good in years," Mimi said.

"Girl, please! Good night, baby." John kissed Mimi's lips.

"John, I love you. Good night," Mimi said.

***

Keshia grabbed her phone off the table and dialed Boogie's number. After four rings, Boogie answered the phone.

"What's up?" Boogie said in a soft tone, not knowing who was calling him from a 305 number.

"Hey, this Keshia. You snitching out here on the streets now? That's what I heard? How you get out of jail before my brother K.B.? He is still in the county without a bond," Keshia said, her tone deep with suspicion.

"Keshia, I have a job and family out here in these streets. Plus, a nigga like me never been in trouble before with the law," Boogie said.

"The street says you snitching outta here to stay in touch with that bitch Meisha. A nigga would do anything not to lose his bitch and material things in the streets," Keshia said.

"Hold up, bitch. You got me fucked up. I'm a real nigga outta here, since day one I was born. A bitch is my last worry outta here. You a nasty bitch that everybody fucked around with. Hoes like you ain't shit!" Boogie said. "I made my bond and you need to make K.B's. bond. You feel me, bitch?" Boogie asked

"Say, my nigga, it's sad when you get your ass beat in your front yard in front of your family. You a damn snitch, nigga. I'm going to put your ass on social media," Keshia said.

"Okay. Keshia this is what happened to me and K.B. We were riding in his Chevy Caprice down West Rose, going to drop off a package to a white boy on the Westside. K.B. seen the police sitting on the church parking lot watching cars pass by. K.B. was driving over the speed limit at the time before he dropped his cell phone on the floor on the driver's side. He tried to reach down to grab his phone but he ran off the road that fast and the police in the parking lot jumped right behind us. K.B. drove about four blocks, then decided to roll the driver window down and toss a clear bag outta the window. That's why the police to pull us over. Your brother panicked and caused himself to be in jail. Now how much you need to bond K.B. out of the county jail?" Boogie asked.

"Nawl," Keshia replied.

"Rain man. That's me with lots of money, cars, clothes, hoes and businesses around town," Boogie bragged with a smile on his face.

"Alright, nigga. Bye," Keshia said.

"Hello. Hello." Boogie continued to holla through the phone, trying to see if Keshia was still on the phone line.

"Yeah, I'm here listening to you, fool. *Hey* is for animal and not me, fool," Keshia said.

"I never said *hey*," Boogie replied.

"Baby, who is that bitch you talking to on the phone that long to? You don't have to explain shit to nobody but me. Come in here and get some of this pussy. Money makes me cum and not words, baby. I'm ready to cum all over that big dick," Candice said in a sexy voice.

"Here I come, Candice." Boogie was so excited that Candice wanted to fuck him in the middle of the day. He hung up on Keshia and headed into the bedroom, where Candice was lying under the covers.

"Nigga, you acting like you scared of this pussy," Candice teased, pulling the blanket down to reveal her naked body. She reached her left hand and put her finger inside her pussy, moving it back and forth, listening to the sounds of her pussy getting wetter and wetter. "Can you handle this pussy about two hours strong with no break?" Candice asked Boogie.

"We will see." Boogie undressed and jumped into the bed with Candice.

"Damn, you got a huge dick." Candice had grabbed Boogie's dick so quickly that he was in shock. The last time Candice fucked Boogie, he had her sore for many days. They always fucked each other at motels, in a car, and at the trap house. "You hear this pussy?" Candice said as she started jacking Boogie's dick off with her right hand.

"You a freak to the fullest. That's one of the reasons we still together. The sound of your pussy makes this dick nut fast," Boogie said with a smile.

"Lay back, baby, and relax. I'ma make you feel real good," Candice said.

"Go ahead and eat this dick up," Boogie said

Candice started working her tongue and mouth action like her life depended on it, and in her mind, it did. Candice started deep-throating Boogie's dick faster and faster. Candice could tell that Boogie was about to nut any moment. Boogie grabbed her hair with his hand and held her head still so she couldn't move. Next thing Candice knew, her mouth was full of cum.

"Go ahead and swallow like a pro!" Boogie demanded, still grasping her hair tightly.

Candice had no choice but to catch every drop in her mouth. Candice risked choking to death to prove her point to Boogie that she loved him. Once Candice finished, she grabbed a shirt out the drawer to wipe her mouth before she prepared for sleep for the night.

"Damn, you have a nice body. When you got up and got the shirt out of the drawer, I was watching your nice booty," Boogie said.

"Nigga, go to sleep," Candice said.

"Okay. Good night," Boogie said.

Chapter 2

Bee Bee was chilling at the strip club with Buffy and Rambo, watching different bitches perform on stage. Buffy spotted her friend Diamond walking toward the bar.

"Hey, Diamond!" Buffy screamed out.

Diamond turned around, looking for whoever was calling her name so loud in the club.

"Damn, bitch, you screaming my name like that," Diamond said as she walked up to Buffy. "How things been with you out here?"

"Things been okay, as you can see," Buffy said, flashing a smile at her man, Rambo.

"I'm in the club tryna get a connect to move some cocaine to these bitches. You got somebody that can point me in the right direction?" Buffy asked.

"I got you. Give me a minute," Diamond said.

Buffy reached inside her bra, pulled out a clear plastic bag, and opened it.

"See here how this shit looks. It's twenty caps of cocaine which is twenty dollars apiece. But if you sell ten for me, you can have the other ten. That will be an easy two hundred dollars' profit for you in here. Once you done, hit me at this number." Buffy handed Diamond a business card. "Make sure you get at me once you done."

"I will," Diamond said. "I have to run to the back of the room to get dressed because the next five minutes . . . it will be my time to dance on stage," Diamond added. She rushed backstage, balling the plastic bag up in her hand. Once she made it backstage, she opened her palm excitedly, showing her friends the bag of cocaine. One of Diamond's homegirls, Famous, damn near jumped out of her seat when she saw it.

"What's up bitch?" Diamond asked Famous.

"Ah shit! You acting tough now, bitch, since you have a little dope in your hands. Let me see what you have," Famous said. She reached into her bra and pulled out a twenty-dollar bill, and handed it to Diamond.

"Bitch, this shit better be good for twenty dollars, or you going give me my money back on the spot," Famous said. "Take this money, bitch," she added with a mean tone of voice.

Meanwhile, Rambo eased into the back room of the club. Buffy had rushed back to the front to get ready to dance on the stage.

Famous tore the plastic bag open and quickly snorted the whole pack up her nose. Two minutes later, she started looking crazy backstage—jumping up and down like she was at a football game. Rambo stepped closer to help Famous, but before he could react, she was pulling off her clothes piece by piece off her body.

"Girl, quit this shit," Rambo said, eyeing her body.

"Nigga, give me that big dick," Famous moaned as she reached for Rambo's pants and unzipped them.

"Bitch, what are you doing?" Buffy said, rushing back into the backstage to get her lip stick. "Hoe, you thought I was on stage? Nigga, you back here fucking this bitch while I'm making you money here in the strip club!" Buffy snapped.

"Buffy, I wasn't doing nothing to Famous. I was looking for the bathroom and got lost." Rambo said.

"Well, that bitch's hands was all on your dick when I walked in! Maybe she sucked you off so fast you was done before I got here. Five minutes ago, I was right here with Famous," Buffy shot back.

"Rambo, Bee Bee waitin' on you at the bar to buy you a drink. How the fuck we supposed to pull some bitches out this club when your tender dick ass back here trickin' off with Famous?" Buffy asked, shaking her head.

"Baby, you got me fucked up. I ain't fuckin' with this basehead bitch. She high as hell off somethin' right now," Rambo said, grinning. "Matter fact, we need to take this bitch home and smash her ass."

"Nigga, let's go." Buffy grabbed her duffle bag off the floor, dug inside for some clothes, and got dressed. She had decided she wasn't dancing tonight.

Once she was dressed, she yanked Rambo by his shirt and dragged him toward the front door. She didn't even look around before stepping outside, still gripping his shirt.

"Hoe-ass nigga, you got me fucked up right now," Buffy said.

"Bitch, you trippin' over nothing," Rambo shot back.

They reached the car and continued arguing inside.

"How the fuck you gon' act crazy on me, Buffy?" Rambo asked, sitting in the passenger seat, looking irritated.

Buffy ignored him and pulled her phone from her pocket, texting her friend Dee Bo.

"What you doin', baby?" Rambo asked as she kept typing.

"Not shit. Thought I'd check my email while we sittin' here," Buffy said, not looking up.

She put the car in drive and pulled off from the club.

"Where you tryna eat at?" Buffy asked.

"I'm cool," Rambo muttered.

"Well, I gotta stop by Neisha's house to do her hair for the concert Monday. You can take the car, and I'll call you when I'm done," Buffy said.

Buffy put the car in drive leaving the club scene. "Where you trying to go eat at? Buffy asked Rambo.

"I'm cool. Rambo said.

"Well, I'm going have to take a ride by Neisha's house and do her hair so she can go to the concert Monday. You can take the car and I will call you once I'm done." Buffy said.

Rambo had no idea Buffy had this shit plan out—to leave him and give him the car.

"I'm sorry, Buffy. You know I got mad love for you," Rambo said, leaning over and kissing Buffy on the jaw while she was driving. "I love you, Buffy."

"Nigga, your breath smell like you been eatin' ass or that bitch Famous' pussy," Buffy shot back.

"What bitch?" Rambo asked.

"That bitch Famous at the club," Buffy screamed.

"Hoe, you wild. You wanted eat this dick up tonight?" Rambo asked.

"Nawl, I'm cool," Buffy said.

"Okay." Rambo's face changed after that short conversation.

Buffy had passed Neisha's house. She had to turn around because the blue house was on the right.

Rambo wasn't feelin' Buffy at the moment. As soon as she pulled up to the house, the car came to a complete stop. Rambo jumped out, opened the back door, grabbed Buffy's duffle bag from the backseat, and sat it on the ground. Then, without another word, he slid into the driver's seat.

"Damn, why you sat my bag on the ground?" Buffy asked.

Rambo looked at Buffy and smiled. Then, he sped off so fast Buffy couldn't believe it.

Rambo was hurt deep inside. Something didn't sit right with him about Buffy getting out the car at Neisha's house.

Buffy walked upstairs to Neisha's front door.

Knock! Knock! Knock!

"Bitch, I know you in there!" Buffy screamed.

"Who the fuck knockin' that hard on my door like they crazy?" Neisha asked from inside.

"Bitch, it's me—Buffy the head doctor!" Buffy replied.

Neisha opened the door with a smile.

16

"Hoe, what the fuck you doin' with that duffle bag?" Neisha asked. "Let me take this bag, and come on inside." Buffy stepped inside and closed the door behind her.

"Bitch, you still thick as a Snicker in them jeans," Neisha said, looking Buffy up and down with a smirk.

"Neisha, we can do your hair tomorrow morning. Right now, I got too much shit on my mind with Rambo," Buffy said. "I texted him and told him I'ma spend the night here. To be real, your cousin Dee Bo supposed to be meetin' me here to take me back to my crib on the Northside."

"Bitch, you gon' do my hair before you go get some dick," Neisha said. "You a cold freak, Buffy. You can't be runnin' around suckin' and fuckin' everything with a dick, bitch."

"Hoe, you know I'm 'bout my money. I can handle two niggas at one time," Buffy said.

"Bitch, what you mean?" Neisha asked.

"Not takin' two dicks at once, bitch! I mean bein' in two different relationships without the other nigga knowin'. You feel me?" Buffy explained.

"Make that shit clear then. I can't let a nigga damage this lil' pussy," Neisha said.

Knock! Knock!

"Who is it?" Neisha yelled, walking toward the door.

"It's me, Dee Bo. Let me in, it's hot as fuck out here," Dee Bo said.

Neisha opened the door.

"Damn, a bitch tired as hell," Neisha sighed.

"Thank you, Neisha," Dee Bo said.

As soon as he saw Buffy, he ran straight to her, full speed. He hugged her so tight she was out of breath for a minute.

"Damn, I love you, bitch," Dee Bo said.

"I love you too, nigga," Buffy said.

"Let's go to your place. I need to grab my jacket I left there last time we was playin' spades," Dee Bo said, trying not to let Neisha know too much of his business.

"Neisha, we'll be back shortly," Dee Bo added.

"Girl, this nigga crazy as hell, 'cause it's gon' take a long time to handle all this pussy," Buffy joked, grabbing her pussy with her left hand and smirking.

Buffy and Dee Bo had been together for years before Rambo came into the picture.

Meanwhile, Buffy's uncle, Ben, had been in the feds for nine years on a twenty-year sentence. He won his appeal years later and was waiting to be resentenced on federal drug charges. Buffy had been holding him down since the day the judge gave him all that time.

Neisha had been crushin' on Buffy's uncle for a long time.

"Bitch, we 'fit to go to my crib. You dreamin' right now," Buffy said.

"We'll talk to you later, Neisha," Buffy said as she and Dee Bo walked out the door and headed to his car.

"Buffy, we 'fit to go to the spot or straight to the Northside . . . I can tell you ain't feelin' too good," Dee Bo said, watching her closely as he put the car in drive.

"Northside," Buffy said.

Thirty minutes later, they pulled up to Buffy's spot on the Northside. As soon as they got out the car, Buffy unlocked the front door.

Both of them stripped down out of all their clothes to the point shit was heating up fast. Buffy slammed the bedroom door quickly.

"What the fuck you doing, Buffy?" Dee Bo asked.

Buffy started licking Dee Bo's tunnel that led to his favorite part of his body. Buffy's long tongue circled around his large dick but didn't make it quite to it. Buffy felt his bottom moving trying to push his dick toward her mouth.

"Bitch, put your mouth on it, please," he begged as Buffy aligned her lips with his mushroom head.

Buffy sucked the tip of Bo's dick, watching as the big veins protruded down his shaft. His dick jumped against her lips, and she smiled at him. She saw his hands ball into big fat fists against his head.

"Nigga, don't snatch a bitch's long weave off her head," she hummed against his huge dick, making him flinch.

She gathered a good bit of wet spit in her mouth and spat it on his dick—some crazy shit she had seen in a porn movie when she was young. Keeping her lips on his dickhead, she let her saliva glide down his shaft like a splashing waterfall. Her small hands massaged up and down his length while she sucked, making him scream out like a bitch.

He kept coaching her on how he wanted it.

With a mouth full of hard dick, she suctioned her cheeks, moving up and down slowly as she found her rhythm. She was making love to his dick with her mouth the same way his dick made love to her wet pussy. She was a hood freak—the type of woman everybody wanted in their relationship.

Her hands stroked what her mouth couldn't devour, and his thick chest flexed from the sensation. Her lips left his dick as she moved down to suck his nuts—first one, then the other.

His eyes locked onto her face. That nigga looked like his eyes were about to pop out his head, like a fiend smoking crack on a can in a dope house. His mouth hung wide open, but no sound came out. You coulda tossed a quarter straight into his mouth—it was open that wide.

"Baby, what the fuck! You look so fuckin' good with this mule dick in your mouth. This shit crazy," he finally managed to say when his lips started working again.

"Yeah," he moaned. "Fuck, baby. Whatever it is, the answer is yes."

He spread his thighs as wide as the soft bed would allow. As his dick jumped inside her cheeks, she knew he was close. He slid it from her wet mouth and gripped her long hair tight, pulling her soft lips to his, kissing her hungrily. He knew her lips would be swollen later from the way he was going at her.

19

The moans coming from her mouth made her pussy leak like a busted pipe. Wrapping his strong arms around her waist, he flipped them over.

He climbed on top of her, pushing his tongue into her mouth, sucking on it. He sucked, bit, and chewed on her lips like a crazy nigga that just broke out the psych ward. His mouth grabbed onto her neck, sending chills through her body.

This was the layer she needed to pull to succeed—aggression.

Leaving passion marks everywhere his tongue traveled, she had no choice but to surrender to the feeling that was pulling her deeper under his spell.

Trailing down her beautiful body, he suctioned her pretty nipples like they were filled with fresh baby cow milk.

Her hands grabbed the back of his bald head, pushing him deeper between her legs. She jumped from the slight graze of his lips.

"Baby, that feels great," Buffy moaned before kissing the top of his forehead four times.

He looked up at her and smiled.

He eased up a little, but that didn't stop him from sucking, moving from one nipple to the other, driving her crazy. He went further down, kissing her small stomach until he reached her pussy. He sucked in a sharp breath, then his long tongue latched onto her huge clit before his entire mouth devoured her.

"Baby, please," she begged, scratching at him, trying to get him to slow down or let her take a quick two-minute break.

Smack! Smack! Smack!

"No fucking hands, baby, while Daddy eating this wet pussy," he said against her big clit. "Hands above your head—now."

His voice loud, commanding, as her sexy body moved in rhythm, ready to be fucked. It was hard, but she obeyed, putting her small hands above her head and squirming. He had her body on fire—somebody needed to call the local fire department to put the blaze out before someone got hurt.

"Damn, my pussy wet and fat as fuck," Buffy moaned. "Look at this shit, nigga!"

He slurped and sucked on her like it was his favorite piece of cheesecake. One of his fingers slid inside of her pussy—then another one—as she let out a deep, mean moan.

"Mmmm," was all she could moan as she rocked against his face while he fingered her pussy.

He pushed her over the edge, placing his long tongue even deeper inside of her pussy. She was excited to do whatever to whatever he had planned. She just hoped it never came to *that* kind of party.

Hard dick was definitely clouding her judgement. She loved it all. Even if it was for this moment, she would make it last.

But something about his eyes didn't sit well with her, and she had to figure it out soon.

He pulled her out of her thoughts, his clit-thumping tongue working its magic again. She was trying her best to hold on, but she couldn't. Every time his lips grazed her clit, it got more and more sensitive.

He stopped suddenly, climbing up her body like Superman, sprinkling kisses everywhere he could find until he made his way to her hips.

"This pussy tastes good to you, huh?" Buffy asked.

He smiled against her lips as she sucked her juices off his. He loved that freaky shit.

He moaned out of nowhere.

She felt his dick at her opening. He pushed in inch at a time until she started to move a little bit. His girth always made it a little painful, but even more pleasurable.

His initial contact was more —spicy with a little pressure and just enough pain.

21

He started easing out, then back in, giving her slow strokes, but she couldn't get back into it. The dick felt good to her, but shit was going through her mind.

He felt something wasn't right.

Without a word, he stopped, grabbed his clothes, got dressed, and headed for the front door.

He thought she would come behind him.

"Fuck you, bitch!" she yelled when the front door closed behind him.

Tears rolled down her face at a fast pace.

Her mouth and pussy were sore from all the pain she took from his large dick inside her.

She laid down for about twenty minutes before grabbing her belongings to take a hot shower.

Dee Bo walked out onto the front porch and noticed the hood was alive with activity that will blow your mind.

Bitches were sucking dick on the side of the house where he was standing.

Drug dealers selling drugs on every block.

Niggas was shooting dice next door.

He walked to his big-body Benz and started it up, as people rushed to his car to buy drugs. He made several small drug sales, counting his money, not paying attention to what was going on around him.

Out of nowhere, a black minivan pulled up. The side door slid open slowly.

Dee Bo's instincts kicked in.

Something wasn't right.

His eyes followed the nigga that got out the van first.

Everything felt like slow motion.

The van came to a complete stop as several niggas piled out.

A lone gunman—dressed in all-black with a ski mask— crept up on the side of Dee Bo's Benz.

"Bo," a woman screamed.

She quickly leaned over toward the steering wheel and slammed her hand on the horn.

Just as the loud horn pierced the air, the masked man with the handgun ran up behind her and opened fire.

Debo was helpless.

He watched the woman opening the door and fall on the ground, crawling for help, but the gunman was unrelenting.

The masked man stood over her and repeatedly shot her.

Her body jerked with every bullet tearing into her flesh.

Tears filled Dee Bo's eyes.

His screams were stuck in his throat.

The masked man ran back to the van and jumped in with the rest of the goons.

As the van passed Dee Bo, the gunman pulled off his mask.

Dee Bo turned in the van's direction.

Through the window, his face was clear.

Her body lay still.

Dee Bo slammed the Benz into drive and sped off at full speed.

He couldn't believe his Benz could go that fast.

Chapter 3

Coca stood on the side of the dance floor at *Club Thunder*, sipping several glasses of vodka while scanning the club scene. Her friend Eve was dancing with her boyfriend, Boogie, who gripped her thick ass cheeks with his hands.

Eve had on a short pink *BabyPhat* skirt—with no panties on.

Boogie slid his large hand under her skirt. Eve's face twisted into a strange expression that puzzled Coca for a moment. Boogie pulled his hand out and stuck his fingers in his mouth before reaching back under her skirt, fingering her pussy again.

Suddenly, he grabbed her small frame and tossed her on the dance floor on her backside. Her skirt flew up, exposing a bald-headed pussy to everyone watching.

Boogie reached down, unzipped his jeans, and pulled out his huge dick.

Coca rushed to the scene. "Get the fuck off her now, nigga!" Coca screamed.

"This bitch belongs to me, as you can see. We are having a little fun before we leave for her birthday."

He tried to continue, but Coca refused to let it go down like that. Boogie was looking sad at the moment.

Coca reached inside her Chanel purse, pulling out a thick piece of metal.

Crack!

Coca smashed Boogie across the head several times.

"Nigga get off her now, bitch."

She hit Boogie again and again, making him fall over. His eyes instantly shut. Coca jumped off the dance floor, running to her best friend. She squeezed Eve's body tight, crying. Eve clutched her skirt down, then suddenly took off running to the women's bathroom. Coca followed, tears still pouring down her face.

Inside the bathroom, the bright lights bounced off the mirrors, creating a beautiful scene.

"Thank you, Coca," Eve whispered, her voice trembling. "I didn't realize that nigga was taking advantage of me while I had several drinks at the bar." Eve looked sad when she said it. "Coca, Boogie claimed he loved me, but he just wanted to show out in front of everybody," Eve said.

"Yeah, Eve, Boogie did make you look bad, but a bitch like me had your back all the way. Now let's go before a bitch catch a case in here. Bitch, you do have a big camel toe down there." Coca laughed, trying to lighten the mood.

"Hoe, quit joking with me all the damn time." Eve smirked, then raised up her skirt, sticking her long middle finger inside her pussy, letting out a loud moan as she moved her finger back and forth several times. Then, she pulled her finger out and slipped it into her mouth.

"Nasty bitch, you eating your old pussy," Coca said. We need to leave right now before the police get here. That nigga is hurt bad in there on the dance floor."

Coca snatched Eve by the hand, dragging her out of the bathroom toward the front entrance. The music was still bumpin'—nobody even noticed them leaving the club.

"That's cool. But don't try no freaky shit with me neither with your beautiful ass. I heard you be fucking them hoes with a huge strap-on around town," Eve said.

"Eve, you crazy as fuck," Coca laughed, kissing Eve on the lips.

They made it to Coca's car and headed to her spot. Eve had too many drinks to think straight—she didn't know what was in store for her.

Twenty minutes later, they arrived at Coca's crib. Coca opened the passenger door, helping Eve out the car by holding her hand.

They started making their way toward the front door, walking like two old ladies.

"Hold up, bitch!" Eve said, kicking her red heels off one at a time onto the ground. Now barefoot, she picked up the pace.

"These niggas out here got a bitch fucked up, tryna fuck on me. They can eat this fat pussy!" Eve reached under her skirt, rubbing her pussy until she lost her balance and fell onto the front porch.

"Damn, Coca, help a bitch up! Where my heels at, bitch?"

"Eve, girl . . . a bitch got you."

Coca pulled her up, then ran to grab her heels off the ground. When she got back, she dug into her purse, looking for her house keys. After four minutes of searching, she finally found them and unlocked the door.

Eve stumbled inside, flopping onto the living room floor with her legs wide open.

Coca closed the front door and headed to the bedroom, grabbing a small box from under the bed—her special stash of sex toys.

By the time Coca came back, Eve was butt-ass naked on the couch bed. Her skirt and the rest of her clothes lay scattered on the floor.

Eve's pussy was shaved bald—a pretty sight to see.

"Damn, bitch! You the new Megan Thee Stallion out here. I see why these niggas go crazy over you."

Eve laughed. "Bitch, come taste this pussy," she said.

Coca grabbed Eve's soft body, lifting her in the air, palming her ass cheeks apart as she bounced her up and down on her while standing.

Coca paused for a second, reaching into the small box and pulling out the nine-inch pink strap-on. She strapped it on fast.

Eve tried to move her hips in a circle but failed miserably—Coca was in control.

All Eve could do was hold on for the long ride. She looked down, watching her wet pussy explode all over Coca's strap-on dick, her tight muscles gripping against the long rubber shaft.

Coca's head fell back as she bounced Eve harder and harder, until Eve's pussy busted, sending a huge splash of cum down Coca's thighs.

Eve moaned like crazy, with her breasts pressed against Coca's chest combined with her sucking, biting and squeezing Coca's neck. Coca tilted her head back, pulling away slightly to look into Eve's eyes. She watched as Eve's eyes slowly opened, then closed again.

Eve looked back into Coca's eyes when she opened them again. They were red and glossy, but that didn't stop Coca from pushing that tight pussy to the limit.

Coca felt Eve's little chest rising and falling sharply—she was breathing hard as fuck, like she was about to pass out at any moment.

"This dick so damn good, bitch!" Eve screamed out in loud pain.

"You brought the best out of a bitch tonight," Coca said as she started pounding away, hitting every wall Eve had in her pussy.

Eve was screaming, crying, cussing, and scratching— Coca was fucking her into another world. By the time Eve *came* three more times from the good sex, Coca had fucked her into a deep sleep.

They lay on the bed, holding each other's soft bodies.

All they could do was hold each other after a long night at *Club Thunder*.

Coca smirked to herself. "This fucking is something Eve will never forget for the rest of her lifetime."

Eve lay beside Coca, knocked the fuck out.

"Yes, a bitch killed that little pussy tonight, bitch." Coca said. She smiled as she closed her eyes to get some rest.

***

Two days later, Buffy sat in her front yard on Maple and Ash Street, counting the money she made that day from selling drugs. She had to make sure she had all of Vimp's money before she could get another package from him. But the little profit she made wasn't enough for her to maintain the fun she enjoyed. Buffy sold a little pussy in the hood to several dope boys every once in a while to make ends meet. Her head game was off the scale.

Buffy walked back into the trap house, but something caught her attention. Her best friend, Shellia, was getting fucked right in the middle of the living room floor. The sounds of the moans made Buffy turn her head after a quick glance at them as she walked right past them, heading into the kitchen.

They noticed Buffy—but they kept fucking like dogs and cats in heat.

"Damn, this pussy great, Shelia. Can you put this dick down your throat?" Silk asked. Silk raised up off of Shelia. He was so deep inside her pussy all you could hear is wet sounds of pussy through the air.

"Baby mama right here will do anything for you at this moment, young nigga," Shelia said, grabbing Silk's dick with her small hands, stroking it back and forth while looking into his eyes. She could tell he was about to cum any second.

"How you like this?" Shelia asked. Shelia was trying to keep Silk from nutting too fast.

"You're the best thing God made in this world." You could tell by the look in Silk's eyes that Shelia's head game had a nigga feeling good at the moment.

Shelia grabbed Silk head, kissing him directly in the mouth. She reached down, grabbing his dick, and placed it in her mouth. She deep-throated him the first few times before her mouth got so wet that spit started dripping onto the floor.

She stopped for a second, then moved down to his nuts, sucking them like a pack of hard candy.

"Baby, you like this freaky shit?" Shelia asked.

"It's okay. Let me put this dick inside your *garage?*" Silk asked.

He grabbed Shelia by her long hair, turned her around, bent her over, and slid his thick dick inside her.

Shelia let out a loud moan that gave Silk even more energy to pound her harder and harder with every stroke.

"Baby, you hurtin' this little pussy! You know a bitch can't take all this dick in my stomach. Please take your time with this pussy."

But after a few more strokes, Shelia started throwing her ass back at him like she couldn't feel the pain anymore.

"Ahh, shit, nigga! I'm about to cum—fuck—ah, fuck!" Shelia screamed out.

"Hold up, that's not what I want you to do right now, Shelia."

Silk turned her around, placing her on her backside and spreading her legs apart.

Then he dived between her legs like he was diving into the ocean.

His tongue hit her big clit, making her jump as he rolled his tongue around her pearl several times before shoving it deep inside her pussy, stroking it back and forth.

He was fucking her with his tongue so hard she couldn't stop moving, screaming loud as hell.

Buffy came back into the living room, irritated.

"Bitch, stop all that screaming! Take that dick like a real woman. You shouldn't have gave him the pussy if you couldn't handle the pain."

Buffy walked out the front door to handle some business.

Silk kept stroking Shelia until she finally gave in and let him do whatever he wanted to her body.

Then he pulled his dick out and slid it into a dark hole.

Shelia screamed out in pain as he went all the way in.

Silk stroked faster, fucking her tight ass until he busted deep inside her hot, wet asshole.

"Nigga, I can't take no more of this pain! You punished me for the last time like this!"

Shelia lay on the floor, drenched in sweat, her asshole still wet.

This bitch Shelia was something else when it came to sex.

But she wasn't used to getting her ass stretched out by a huge dick.

"Baby, come hold a bitch, please . . . or get me my clothes over there?" Shelia asked.

Silk reached over to the black chair and handed Shelia her clothes. She decided not to put on her panties, instead slipping them into her purse.

"Damn, is that pussy that wet that you can't put your panties back on?" Silk laughed.

"Fuck you, nigga," Shelia said in a mean voice. "I gotta go home, take a shower, and I'll holla at you tomorrow sometime."

Shelia finished getting dressed, then kissed Silk on the lips before walking out the front door.

"Nasty bitch," Silk muttered as Shelia disappeared outside.

He went into the guest bedroom, grabbing some fresh clothes to take a quick shower—just in case another bitch came over and wanted some dick.

***

Buffy pulled up to Vimp's crib and got out of her car. She knocked on the front door several times; nobody answered. Frowning, Buffy reached inside her front pocket, pulled out her cell phone, and dialed Vimp. The phone rang three times. No one picked up. Buffy glanced at the driveway. Vimp's car was still parked out front. It was strange nobody came to the front door or even answered the phone. Buffy decided to walk around the house and she saw something strange like never before. The side window was raised up, and a tall black chair was placed outside the window on the ground, like someone used it to climb into the house through the window.

"Oh my god!" Buffy's stomach dropped as she peeked through the window.

Inside, Vimp lay on the floor with a knife stuck in his chest.

Blood was dripping from his forehead.

Her first instinct was to run inside, but fuck that—she wasn't about to get caught up in some bullshit.

Instead, she turned around and walked back to her car.

Pulling out her phone, she called Silk.

"Hello," Silk answered groggily, sounding like he had just woken up.

"Someone murdered Vimp!" Buffy yelled through the phone

Click!

Silk hung up. He walked into the bedroom and get dressed after stepping out of the shower. About ten minutes later, he heard someone scream for help from the top of their lungs. He looked out the bedroom window and was surprised to see Buffy walking on the front porch. Buffy had a lot on her mind because she wasn't feeling Dee Bo anymore in their relationship, but on the inside, you could tell something wasn't right because Buffy spent a lot of time at the trap spot with Silk.

Silk rushed to put his clothes and shoes on, but before he knew it . . .

"Somebody killed Vimp! Yes, he is dead." Buffy burst into the bedroom, still yelling.

"Calm down, damn!" Silk said, looking her dead in the face. His expression turned serious. "Shit is crazy out here right now," he muttered.

Silk grabbed Buffy, wrapped his strong arms around her body, as tears continued to fall down her cheeks. "Come on, let's go back to Vimp's crib and see what the fuck is going on."

They ran outside and jumped in Buffy's car.

Buffy hesitated before putting the car in drive.

"Niggas been tryna kill Vimp for years on the Westside. I told him to stop fuckin' with them niggas, but he did anyway."

A thousand thoughts ran through Buffy's head as she pressed her foot on the gas.

"Just chill, Buffy. We gon' get to the bottom of this real soon," Silk reassured her.

They arrived at Vimp's crib thirty minutes later. A man in a white jacket stood on the front porch. It seemed that the man was smoking something in one hand and holding a large handgun in the other hand.

Buffy's eyes narrowed.

"What the fuck this nigga doing, baby?" Buffy asked.

Silk leaned forward in his seat, looking out the passenger window. The man flicked his assumed blunt onto the ground.

"Buffy I'm thinking about shooting this nigga on the spot— no questions asked," Silk said coldly.

Without hesitation, Buffy put the car in reverse.

"Fuck that, let's go," she said, talking shit as she sped toward her main spot. She drove a few blocks down and pulled into the corner store in the hood. She left enough space between them and Vimp's crib so she could still see the front porch. Buffy and Silk weren't blood-related, but they had grown up together in the hood and called each other family. From where they sat, they were sure the nigga on the porch couldn't see them. Not only was it broad daylight outside, but they were idling pretty far away.

Silk squinted. "Can you see that bitch-ass nigga from here still?" Silk asked, leaning forward, trying to see over Buffy's shoulder.

Buffy kept her eyes locked on the scene.

"Yeah, I see 'em walking off the front porch, getting into his car," Buffy said. Silk passed Buffy a 9mm handgun and kept his eyes on the target.

The man pulled off from the house.

"Baby let's get the hell away from the scene before the police get here." Buffy's voice was low, almost a whisper.

She put the car in drive and peeled off.

They headed to their crib for the night.

Chapter 4

The next morning, Buffy woke up watching Silk, who was still sleeping. Buffy was tempted to give him the standard treatment, which consisted of her mean head game, but she was skeptical after how distant he was the other night with Shelia. Even after they got back on track, Buffy took a hot shower, oiling her body up this morning. She came out the shower, naked with clean skin, and that nigga rolled over, shut his eyes, didn't breathe in her direction at all in that moment. That bullshit shut Buffy's self-esteem down. Buffy didn't know if she could take a letdown coming from a nigga she thought would never break her heart.

"Fuck it! Let a bitch order something to eat from Perkins." Buffy said. She was tired of staring at Silk's hard dick, as if it was going to make it move. She got out the bed to quench her stomach hunger.

"Get back in the bed, Buffy." Silk scared the fuck outta Buffy.

"Huh?" Buffy replied.

"You heard me, back in the bed," Silk said.

Buffy had no intention of refusing his request, seeing every muscle ripple against the sheets. She crawled back in bed, headed to her favorite position to give what she figured he loved the most.

"Nah, sweetie, a nigga need to be inside your guts right now," Silk said. Silk wanted to let off some frustration and shoot up the club, cumming inside her pussy. He pulled her close to him, tossing her on the bed. He inserted his dick inside her deeper than she thought, pounding and pounding inside her pussy. Releasing the anxiety he had over seeing his ex-girlfriend losing her life all in one night at a party again.

"Oh shit, big dick nigga!" Buffy screamed to the beat, loving the strokes he was putting on her pussy. Buffy figured Silk had gotten over whatever had him in a fucked-up mood, and she played her cards right by not stressing him, but taking the pain from his dick.

"I need your dick in my mouth," Buffy said.

Silk slid his dick out of her pussy, slipped it inside her mouth, and continued his strokes as his anger began subsiding with each vigorous thrust. Buffy clawed her long nails into his back, down to his solid, hard ass, pushing him further inside her mouth until it felt as if his long dick was about to shoot up in her deep throat.

"Nigga, a bitch loved this dick!" Buffy purred, thinking that her bomb-ass pussy was the reason for the hard pounding her pussy was getting earlier. She could feel his body throbbing, praying that he would cum inside her. "Baby, c—cum . . . inside me!" she managed to say, dying for him to bless a seed inside her. He shot cum all down her throat like he was shooting an AR-15 with several rounds let loose. Buffy licked every drop of cum and wrapped her arms around Silk, falling into a deep sleep.

"Damn baby, you're the best. Your head game is one thousand strong." He stared at her while she was sleeping. He could not believe she was that damn thick naked. "You're not going back to that nigga," Silk laughed to himself in deep thought. Silk hissed over Buffy's body, taking in the sight of how beautiful she really was. He spread open her ass and pierced the back of her pussy with his engorged dick. Buffy was in a deep sleep. All of a sudden, words started coming out of her mouth: "Fuck me, my daddy . . . yes . . . take this pussy . . . aaah . . . mmm . . . ooohh . . ." She couldn't go another minute without the stretch of a dick inside her pussy.

Now Silk was behind her, pleasing her, fucking into her pussy like a wild man, horny nigga. Buffy clenched around Silk, and he groaned in pleasure as she came around his dick fast. He pulled out, leaving the crown of his dick slick and swollen, the rubber already filled with pre-nut. He wanted to feel her naked pussy on his dick, skin-to-skin. But she wouldn't allow it. He sank to his knees and long-tongued her ass, greedily licking the poking rim as he slid several fingers into her pussy. His tongue lashed over her hole, then darted around it as his probing fingers found her spot and stroked its swollen heat. Buffy was fully aware of everything going on at the moment.

Buffy mewled, clawed at her sheets on the bed, her long nails raking viciously over the surface. "Suck my big clit," she demanded, her need rolling out into a whisper. She arched her back like a mean cat, spread her legs wider, reached back, and pulled open her ass cheeks, allowing him access and privilege to all of her swollen sex.

Silk took in the magnificence of her cunt, her labia, her slit, her scent, then positioned himself beneath her, her sex hovering over his face. He opened his drooling mouth and latched onto her clit and sucked it in.

"Ahhh Silk . . . bite it," she pushed out, laying her clit bare.

Silk slid his long tongue from her core to her clit. Then, with teeth and tongue, he nipped at the swollen bud, then grazed it, scraping her with pleasure until, finally, biting into it. Heat and sparks shot from her clit, then gushed out from her slit, soaking Silk's face with her desire.

Buffy cupped her breasts, tweaked her beautiful nipples until they ached. She closed her thighs around Silk's head and rode his face like a black cowgirl at a black rodeo. He groaned like a bulldog, grabbing his dick, slowly stroking himself. Her pussy was so luscious, so heavenly. Lost in the throes, he licked and sucked, nibbled and bit.

Silk ravished her sex, filling her with desire, her sweaty body tightening, then going slack, then rigid all over again with need. Another climax crashed against Buffy's walls, splashing out in heavy waves of bliss as expletives filled the bedroom, and her body convulsed, her pussy melting into her young lover's mouth.

Mouth curling up in a satisfying smile, Silk was ready to plunge back inside her wet, slippery pussy. Veins hummed in his body for release, for her. He needed to get back inside her now. Quick on his feet, his erection bobbed up and down in anticipation. An instant later, Silk's dick was at the opening of her slit again, his head aching for entry past swollen tissues, back into her juicy flesh.

Buffy drew in a breath as Silk touched her, using his fingers to open her wide, making her more needy, more aroused. Then she inhaled, feeling the plump head of his dick at her entrance, all slick, all ready, wanting him, waiting for him. Her fat pussy clenched with emptiness. She longed to have him back inside her.

"Bury your dick deep inside me," Buffy said, in a voice heavy with lust and tears. "Lose yourself inside me, my baby," Buffy said.

Silk moaned out loud. Oh, how he wanted back inside her so desperately, lost in her sweet heat! Without words, he gave himself what she asked for. Between gnashed teeth, he gave himself what he craved. What they both craved. His big dick went deeper inside her wet pussy. Silk's small toes curled. Buffy grew wetter, her swollen lips wrapping around his dick with each thrust into her body, her cunt quaking with joy. Exploding. Clenching. Dick drawing out, then plunging in, drawing out, then plunging in. In. Out. In. Out.

Rhythmic pounding lifted Buffy's body up with every thrust. Her walls tightened. Delicious pleasure soared through her soft body, clutching, crashing, and colliding into Silk's own crippling need.

"Feel that," Buffy rasped. "My wet pussy for you, baby. My needy pussy is greedy for you," Buffy said.

Silk moaned loud. "Aaah shit, yes baby, yeah baby . . ." He thrust deeper, faster, and harder. "Shit!" The friction and heat were making him mindless. Buffy pushed back against Silk, her ass slamming against his grain.

"Faster! Harder! Faster!" Buffy said.

Silk groaned, bucking faster, sawing his dick back and forth, in and out, his swollen dick pillaging her core. Buffy heard herself crying out in pleasure. Heard the slap of Silk's body against hers.

Silk quickly pulled out. Moments later, Buffy was pulling her legs back, her knees pressing toward her breasts, , gazing up at Silk as he slapped the swollen head of his dick against her wet cunt.

"Yes, my darling," Buffy cooed, pulling open her sensitive folds. "Cum all over my butt. Let me feel your heat . . ." Buffy said.

"Ohh fuck!" Dazed at the sight of her pink inside clenching and quivering, her juices pooling out, Silk choked back a yell as heavy ropes of scorching cum gushed from his dick, lapped against her labia, and singed her clit. Silk was excited, pumping himself over and over. He squeezed his dick, releasing ribbon after ribbon of his seed, emptying his swollen sack. He pumped himself, milking the cum out, every last drop, until he had nothing else left.

Buffy moaned as Silk laid his steel-hard dick over her slit and slid back and forth over it, before sliding its head over her sex and slathering his warm milky seed into her flesh.

"Lick me," Buffy hissed, her thick hips slowly undulating. Buffy said in a sexy tone of voice.

Tongue out, Silk leaned in and buried his face between her thighs, licking her clean for about ten minutes. Buffy came all over again.

"Wow!" Silk screamed out. Ten minutes later, they fell asleep holding each other. Both of them were tired from all the positions they performed to get to the next level and fall asleep for a good night's rest.

Chapter 5

Jade was coming home from a long day on the block selling drugs. Jade stood frozen, her hand still clasping the doorknob. Her breath was caught somewhere between her chest and her lips, suspended in the chill air of disbelief. The home that had always been her sanctuary was now the stage for her greatest betrayal, and she was the unwilling audience to a tragic play. Jade dropped her Chanel bag. Standing in front of the bedroom, hearing the moaning from a woman, she opened the bedroom door. "Bitch get the fuck outta my house now!" Jade screamed. Her initial reaction was to drag the woman lying on her back out of the bed, but seeing the horrific shock on the woman's face in the bed made her quickly re-asses that decision. Jade and the other woman both seemed to be stuck on a pause, and the only person being on fast forward was a nigga, who continued getting his stroke on as if nothing was going to stop him from busting a nut.

"Oh shit! A nigga almost about to cum," he yelled. He moaned with the sheet over his head hiding his face, but you could believe it was Jade's husband fucking another bitch right in front of her face in their home. Immediately, flashback images consumed her. She couldn't bear the thought that the bullshit she had seen happening right on her matrimonial bed was her husband, entwined with the silhouette of another woman. Their whispers were a cacophony in her ears, their laughter mocking symphonies that swirled around the room, stinging Jade's heart with each careless giggle.

In the chasm of heartache, from the throes of abandonment, Jade felt something erupt within her a dark and seething torrent of anger. Before she knew it, her hand reached for the crystal vase perched innocently on the foyer table. With the elegance of a dance and the violence of a storm, Jade hurled the vase towards the unsuspecting lovers. The sound of shattering glass mirrored the fracturing of her world. The lovers, startled and drenched in petals and water, disentangled themselves from their compromising position. They stared, mouth agape, at the figure of Jade, whose eyes blazed with fury, face hardened into an unreadable mask. There was no room for words, no space for excuses. The air itself seemed to recoil from the scene. Without a second glance, Jade turned away. She left the broken vase, the shattered dreams, and the fragments of her heart scattered on the floor behind her as she walked out.

In a haze she packed a small suitcase. Her movements were mechanical, robotic—the result of a mind trying to protect itself from the agony that loomed like a specter. The hotel lobby was a blur as Jade checked in, her fingers trembling as she signed her name with a flourish that betrayed her inner turmoil. The room she entered was nondescript, a sanitized space that offered her nothing but the solitude she craved. She didn't bother to unpack. Instead, she sat on the edge of the bed, staring out at the city that suddenly felt foreign.

Many hours passed, marked only by the fading light seeping through the curtains. And then, there was a knock on the door. Jade contemplated the possibility of ignoring it, but curiosity—or perhaps fate—coaxed her to stand and open the door. As it turned out, the knock she thought she'd heard hadn't been on her door. Across the hallway, there had been a commotion, a gentleman struggling with an overpacked suitcase and a door that wouldn't budge. The stubborn lock gave in just as Jade emerged, and their eyes met, a silent acknowledgment of the day's victories and defeats hanging between them. He was the antithesis of her husband's kind eyes that held stories instead of secrets, and a confronting smile that hinted at solace, not seduction. They exchanged pleasantries, the simplicity of the interaction belying the complexity of the emotions beneath.

Over the next day, they saw more of each other—'two strangers finding a strange solace in the coincidences that brought them together. Conversation revealed shared interests and mutual understanding. The hotel, once a place of retreat, became an arena for healing. Jade would never forget the scene she'd walked into, the night that changed everything. But as she laughed at a joke her new friend had made, she hoped that the worst moments of her past could indeed lead to new beginnings. From the ashes of betrayal, Jade began to forge a new path, one that led away from vengeance and towards a future filled with hope. She never forgot, but she learned to forgive not him, but herself. And in that forgiveness, she found the strength to move on, into the arms of life, the embrace of a man who had been merely a stranger across the hallway.

Jade and her hallway acquaintance, who she now knew as Ethan, became fixtures in each other's transient hotel lives. Their initial casual interactions evolved into shared meals, thoughtful conversations, and laughter that filled the empty spaces in each other's recent pasts. Both were healing from their wounds, and they found each other a kindred spirit. Ethan, too, had his share of shadows. He had come to the hotel to escape the relentless pace of a career that demanded everything and gave back nothing but emptiness. His encounter with Jade was unexpected, a spark of light in a world that had become too dim.

Weeks turned into months, and the hotel turned from a shelter to a crossroads for two lives intertwined. The staff began to recognize them, two individuals slowly stitching a tapestry of companionship with every passing day. One evening, as they sat beside the hotel's rooftop pool, their feet dangling into the water, Jade felt the last barriers around her heart crumble. The city lights played across Ethan's face, casting him in an ethereal glow.

"Ethan," Jade began, her voice a whisper lost in the city's breath, "I don't know how to thank you for being here. You've seen me at my worst, and you never once walked away."

Ethan turned to her, his hand finding hers in the water, their fingers knitting together with ease. "Jade, being here with you has given me a reason to pause to see that there's more to life than the corner office and the endless chase. You've given me perspective."

Their conversation meandered through dreams deferred and hopes reignited until the night sky began to pale at the edges. It was then, as the first light of dawn brushed the horizon, that Ethan's hand gently tilted Jade's chin towards him. Their lips met, not with the fire of raw passion, but with the softness of rain on parched earth—a kiss that spoke of new beginnings and tender possibilities.

The hotel that had borne witness to their individual pains now stood sentinel over their budding relationship. In time, they moved out, first into a shared apartment bathed in the warm light of recovery, and eventually into a house that echoed the sound of laughter and life. His muscle was built in all the right spots. Every time the light flashed, Jade noticed how breathtaking he was. He licked his lips. Jade wasn't sure if the sensual gesture was directed at her or not, but she battered her thick lashes over her green eyes and gave him a mischievous beautiful smile anyway, before slowly pivoting on her "fuck-me" heels, giving him her round ass stare. His blood was pumping in his dick.

Jade eased her hand down into his waistband of his underwear, fingered the dark curly thatch around his thick dick. His erection pulsed in her hand, thick and ready. She moaned at the feeling of his impressive size. His dick was hard as a brick. She wanted him. Now. She yanked his underwear down over his hips. They leaned in and crushed their mouths together, kissing passionately. Her beautiful eyes twinkled as she stroked his dick with a gloved hand. She licked her lips, then took her hand and massaged him with both her hands. "I want you deep in my cunt," she said, wrapping her gloved hand around his big nuts and the base of his large dick. "Would you like that?" she asked.

He moaned out his answer as she grabbed his erection by the base, sliding her gloved hands up and down his dick. She brought her lips to his neck, biting the skin over his jugular. The bite turned into a sexual lick, then a kiss, then another bite. Pre-nut slid out from the tip of his dick, dripping onto her hand. She lifted her hand to her mouth, licking over her glove.

"Mmm," she urged as she lifted her hand to his mouth. He licked her hand, moaned, then licked over her glove again. She grabbed his nuts and stroked him again until pre-nut streaked her glove. She let go of his turgid flesh, then playfully slapped his face before sliding in front of him and rolling her thick hips until she was positioned directly in front of his perfectly straight dick, pointing rigidly like an arrow at its target.

She bent over, pulled her thong to the side, and then eased back, fucking herself on his dick, raw and filthy, looking around the room.

He grabbed her small ankles, thrusting deep inside her pussy again and again. He slammed his dick inside her so hard, sliding in and out of her pussy. Feeling heat sweep over her body, Jade cried out, looking up into the burning eyes of a familiar face walking into the bedroom. She forgot to lock the front door. All of a sudden, the person disappeared. Her eyesight wasn't clear from all the pain, stress, and fucking she took from Ethan's dick. She had a flashback to killing her husband, but it was only a thought. Her mind was lost from her husband cheating on her with another bitch in their home.

"Are you okay, Jade?" Ethan asked.

"Yes. Just here thinking about how good the sex was with you," Jade said.

"Okay, let me get dressed and head back to work. If you need anything, please let me know. You got some good pussy, baby girl," Ethan said.

"You have a huge dick. You know this pussy is tight, and a bitch ain't a young woman anymore, as you can see," Jade said.

He laughed as he walked out of the room to his car. "Damn, that bitch fine," Ethan said.

Jade gathered her belongings together, and went to take a hot shower. She heard a loud sound at the front door. "Who is it?" Jade asked. She opened the front door with a surprised look on her face. The woman kissed Jade straight on the mouth—she hadn't seen Jade in years since high school.

The strange thing about this woman was that she was none other than Buffy at the door, who Jade had thought was a man earlier, wearing a baseball cap and sunglasses.

Buffy licked her lips at the sight of Jade's body, imagining herself undressing and sliding her body down Jade's pussy.

Buffy had a small box in her hands that she carried around on special trips. Buffy entered the house, placing the small box on the floor next to where she took a seat on the couch to chill out for a minute. Jade had on hardly any clothes. She was about to take a quick shower before someone knocked at the front door.

"What's good, Jade?" Buffy asked.

"Not shit. Just missed the hell outta you at times," Jade said.

Buffy reached down into her small box, grabbing a long piece of plastic, which seemed to be a strap-on.

"Damn, bitch, that's a big one there. Who you been using that shit on?" Jade asked. Jade slapped her pussy with her

45

small left hand. "Let me see you put that strap-on, baby," Jade said.

Buffy pulled down her clothes, putting the strap-on on fast. "I'm going to get naked to the fullest for you, friend. This is about nine inches of hard plastic, but it's my big dick. How you like me now?" Buffy asked, holding the plastic in her hand.

"Girl, that's a huge dick," Jade smiled.

"Oh, yes, baby," Buffy replied. Buffy then kissed Jade directly on the mouth again, causing her eyes to roll in the back of her head this time. Buffy's lips were on her neck, quickly nipping at Jade's flesh. Buffy's head ducked down, licked her nipples, then sucked her tongue back into Jade's mouth.

"Yes, baby," Jade said with excitement.

"Hold your body tight," Buffy said. Buffy stuck her long middle finger inside Jade's panties, getting her pussy even wetter. Jade moaned with veins popping through her forehead. Buffy spread Jade's legs wide open, then sunk deep inside. The first three strokes made Jade scream and moan loud, the sounds echoing through the house.

"Harder! Faster! Harder! Yes, yes . . . give me more dick."

Buffy stopped for a second, putting her mouth on Jade's pussy. Buffy flicked her tongue in and out, causing Jade's pussy to flood her mouth with pre-nut. Jade rocked her hips as Buffy sucked the life outta her pussy. "Baby, you're the best," Buffy stated.

"Baby, put that strap back on me in special places," Jade said. Jade moaned again. "Ahh shit, bitch! I'm cuming on this tongue. Ah shit, bitch, here it come!" Jade came all in Buffy's face, her body shaking like a car running out of gas before making it to the gas station.

"Damn, you taste good, Jade," Buffy said.

"Thank you," Jade replied. They both laid down to get a night's rest.

Chapter 6

Three days later, Jade's heels clicked against the shiny marble floor of the bank. Dark shades covered her eyes as she stood behind a small counter, acting as if she was filling out a deposit or withdrawal slip. She carefully transcribed the note Buffy had provided, word for word, onto the bank's withdrawal slip. She looked around, trying not to show her nerves. She had a precise time to act. If she made one false move, everyone would be thrown off their role. She was the point person, and everything going as planned depended on her. Jade swallowed hard as Buffy walked in, then Rambo, and then her. They fanned out and got into their rehearsed positions. Now, most of the banks were covered and being watched. Jade looked at her watch and exhaled. Ten seconds left. *Slide the paper under the clear glass. Tell the teller, "No funny business," and show her the gun. Slide the paper under the glass.* She continued to rehearse her role over and over again in her head. She also thought about the alternate plan, just in case.

Jade had been charged with shooting the young guard that stood by the customer service tables, running his mouth. If something happened, she would handle this and take the charge for the case. Buffy and Rambo would then take the counters and snatch as much money as they could get. Jade was there just to ensure everything went according to the time frame. She usually had these things mapped out for the best. Eight minutes was all they had from the time they walked in until the time they reached their getaway car. Jade swallowed hard. She felt sweat dripping down the side of her face, and her pussy was soaking wet. The time had finally come. She walked slowly to the middle teller, as instructed. See, Buffy had found out from an insider at the bank that the middle teller didn't have a panic button in front of her station. The teller would either have to lean right or left, which would tell them if she was trying to push the button.

"Good morning, ma'am. How can I help you today?" the teller asked, not really paying too much attention to the customer standing in front of her.

Jade silently pushed the slip of paper under the small opening in the glass. The teller's eyes popped open, and she looked around nervously as soon as she read the words. Now, she was paying attention to the customer standing in front of her.

The teller immediately looked left and locked eyes with Buffy, who smiled at her and patted her waistband to let her know not to try anything funny. Then the teller started to notice the other members around, sticking out like sore thumbs among the regular bank customers.

"Ma'am, how would you like your bills counted out?" the teller asked, trying to remain calm.

"I don't have a preference," Jade coolly replied.

"I have to get some more tens," the teller said. "I will be right back."

Jade figured the teller was probably getting a bag to put the stack of money in, because she had been warned in the note about panic buttons, dye packs, and calling the law.

Buffy watched the teller from a distance. Buffy noticed the teller to her left giving Buffy a little glance. Buffy tapped her foot impatiently. She figured whatever the middle teller had said to Jade was a secret. Then the other teller looked down and reached for something. That was enough for Buffy. She walked over to Jade, who looked up at her as if to say, *What the fuck are you doing, bitch? Are you crazy?*

"Baby, we gotta get outta here. We can stop at another bank on the way out of town," Buffy said, grabbing onto Jade's small arm.

On the way out of town was the signal to leave the scene. Jade quickly followed Buffy's lead and split. When Rambo noticed them rushing out of the back toward the front door, he lost all train of thought. "What the fuck is y'all doing? I ain't leaving outta here without some money!" Rambo screamed loudly, pulling his .40 Glock from his waist.

Screams erupted all over the bank. People began running for the nearest doors, and some got down on the floor.

Meanwhile, a young male security guard tried to draw his weapon, but before he could even hoist it up, one of the crew members shot the security guard dead.

Boom! Boom! Boom! "Let's get the fuck outta here!" Buffy screamed at Rambo.

Jade began running for the door, but the older man— another security guard—tried to grab her. Rambo lit him up with his .40 Glock, and the guard's blood sprayed on Jade's face and clothes, making her sick and weak. The adrenaline was pumping through her body, and she felt like she would faint at any minute. Rambo continued to spray at random and reloaded his .40 Glock for more war.

The inside of the bank was pure pandemonium now, with bodies dropping from his reckless bullets. Rambo jumped up on the counter, but the bullet-proof glass was too high to climb over it. When the tellers had all fled to the bank's emergency robbery shelter, Rambo got so mad, he started shooting more of the bank's customers at random like he was a madman.

Buffy heard the distant wails of sirens. She was finally out the front door of the bank. Whoever wasn't with her would just be left behind. Jade was right behind Buffy, but she started to stumble farther behind. Jade was trying to keep up with Buffy. She kicked off her heels and tried running barefoot, but she was too weak to pick up speed. Buffy knew they had a getaway car waiting for them up the block but hadn't given the driver the signal to come get them from the front of the bank. Rambo took off down the street, but the block was beginning to fill up with cops. Rambo was now hot on Buffy's heels, but Jade had fallen farther back, her chest burning with each step.

"Police! Police! Police! Drop your weapons now!" A cop screamed at them.

Rambo turned and opened fire, hitting the officer right in the forehead.

"Get the fuck in, Rambo!" Buffy screamed out loud.

Jade was still coming toward them, trying hard to make it to the car. Winded, she continued struggling, running for dear life. Jade heard a loud *boom* as the cops opened fire on them, and bullets whizzed by her head. "Wait!" Jade screamed, tears and makeup streaking down her face. It looked like they were leaving her. She was almost there, but then they moved away from her. "What are y'all doing?" Jane screamed. "Buffy!" The faster she ran, the farther away the getaway car moved.

"Do it now, bitch!" Rambo yelled.

Buffy extended her arm out the window and opened fire on Jade. The police were also shooting at Jade.

Jade felt hot metal searing through her skin. Her eyes bulged in shock and pain. Jade was in disbelief that her own cartel family had set her up. As Jade's legs stopped moving, she thought about life and more—the great betrayal she had just suffered. Then she gave up. Her bullet-ridden body lurched forward and hit the ground with a spat. She felt the life leaving her.

"Why, Buffy, why?" Jade screamed as blood spilled from her mouth. Within no time, her limp, lifeless body was surrounded by cops. Buffy and Rambo were in their own vehicle. The getaway driver was still on the scene somewhere, as Buffy and Rambo hit several blocks, leaving the police jumping into another car they had stashed a few blocks away. Buffy knew at least ten people were dead at the bank. Buffy couldn't look back after killing Jade on Rambo's orders to do so. The thought of replacing Jade gave her instant chills down her body.

"Damn, bitch, I thought Jade was your bottom bitch," Rambo said. "Anyways, you had to do what you had to do."

"I know. That bitch was a snake. She was fucking everybody in the streets. We just wanted her to help us get this last big lick before we murked her ass," Buffy said. Rambo didn't have the nuts to stand in front of Jade and kill her himself, so he had instructed Buffy to make sure her death looked like it was a result of a bank robbery gone bad. Buffy still had too much love for Jade. She was in her own world, thinking about her girlfriend—Jade

Rambo remained silent in the opposite direction of the racing police cars.

Buffy was hurting inside.

Chapter 7

Someone was banging at Bambi's door late at night. Bambi grumbled as she rushed to her front door. *Better not be this Jade bitch talking about she forgot something over here last week.* "Who is it?" Bambi yelled.

"Blytheville Police Department!" an officer yelled in a booming baritone voice on the other side of the door.

Bambi screwed up her face and yanked the front door open. She thought maybe Jade had been picked up for something she had done in the past.

"Ms. Williams?" the officer called her last name

"No. My last name is Daniels. My daughter's last name is Williams," Bambi said nervously. A sick feeling washed over her.

"Can we come in?" One of the *laws* asked. Bambi moved aside, and the *laws* stepped into her crib.

"We are so sorry to tell you that your daughter has been murdered," the officer stated to.

Bambi's ears started ringing, and she couldn't move. A scream was welling up inside of her, ready to erupt at any time. She opened her mouth, and the sound that escaped was almost like a chicken at a slaughterhouse. Bambi fell to her knees weak and screamed. "Hell nawl, this shit can't be true!"

The officers tried to help her up, but Bambi wouldn't move from the spot. She was wracked with sobs, and her body trembled. After a few minutes on her knees, wailing uncontrollably, the *laws* finally helped her up.

"What the fuck happened to my baby?" Bambi yelled. "Why it had to be my daughter to die?"

"Your child was shot fleeing from the scene of a nasty bank robbery. Jade was with a group of young thugs that tried to rob the bank," one of the officers informed Bambi.

"You must be mistaken! My child wouldn't do something like that! Jade is a good daughter! Jade knows better than to do wrong. I don't believe shit you saying to me at the moment. Get the fuck outta my house!" Bambi belted out, flailing her small arms at the laws.

"Ms. Daniels, I'm afraid it was your child." The officer showed a picture of Jade's bloodied body to Bambi.

Bambi placed her hand over her mouth. "Oh my God."

"We need you to come down to the hospital and see if this your daughter," the officer said.

Bambi grabbed her coat and car keys off the table and walked out the front door. She was shocked that the police asked her to come to the hospital.

Bambi raced her car through the streets of Blytheville, running all red lights and stop signs on the way to the hospital as her heart beat faster and faster. *I hope my daughter is okay,* Bambi thought to herself.

Twenty minutes later, Bambi arrived at the local hospital. She flew down the hallways, almost knocking people down several times. Bambi noticed a group of law enforcement officers standing in the hall. She rushed over to where they were standing with a sad look on her face.

"Hey, I'm Jade's mother. I was instructed to come to the hospital," Bambi said. She was trying to catch her breath at the same time she was talking.

"Hello. I'm Officer Ted with the Blytheville Police Department." A short Black man extended his right hand for a handshake.

"What's going on with my daughter Jade?" Bambi asked.

"Our initial reports say Jade was shot several times by her friends at the scene of an armed robbery," the officer explained to Bambi.

Bambi broke down in tears. She knew right away who she would make pay for her daughter's death. The goons had taken her only daughter.

Bambi stormed out of the hospital. She needed time to think and regroup about this whole situation.

Once outside, she entered her car and began plotting more on the downfall of their entire team who killed her daughter.

As she pulled off from the hospital, she went home to take a shower and get a nice night of rest.

***

Two weeks later, Bambi sat in the front row at Jade's funeral, hoping she could make it through such a bad day.

Bambi hadn't slept good in two weeks since finding out about Jade's death. Bambi was upset, with killing in her heart. She could hardly stand to look at herself in a mirror.

Bambi always thought of herself as a stand-up bitch at all times. She realized she hadn't been strong enough to stand up to niggas in the hood and say, *Hell no*, when they approached her the first time. She'd been blinded by the money and fearing for her family safety.

Well, things had changed with a bitch she said to herself.

She wasn't afraid anymore. She was pissed and didn't care who thought differently about her. Bambi needed some sort of redemption. Suddenly, it was now her mission to handle her business.

The funeral was over, and Bambi headed home for some rest after thinking about the crew that murdered her daughter for no damn reason.

Chapter 8

Rambo picked Buffy up off her feet. He carried her inside the master bedroom to the king-size bed, laid her down, and studied her naked body as Keith Sweat played in the background. This nakedness was new to him, especially the marks on her lower back that looked like a trade stamp. He massaged her body from her feet to her neck, then across her back, and over her ass cheeks. He massaged her so well that she didn't want him to stop.

Rambo turned Buffy over and massaged her legs up to her breasts, lingering on them as he stared into her eyes. Then, he got naked, and Buffy's mind went dark, consumed by devilish thoughts. She jacked his large dick off. Rambo massaged her pussy in return. Buffy was nervous about the robbery and the death of Jane still hanging in her mind.

"Baby, hold up for a minute." Buffy stroked him with both hands, then took him in her mouth, making his dick disappear down her throat.

"Damn, this mouth's fire," Rambo said aloud, groaning with approval. Buffy pulled his dick out of her mouth.

"Rambo, you love me?" Buffy asked, holding his dick in her hand. It was growing bigger in her small hands.

"Yes," Rambo replied.

That turned Buffy on, and she started crying in disbelief, overwhelmed by the words he said.

Rambo placed his nervous hands on her damp skin, touching each part like it was a separate work of art, not one continuous sculpture. He kissed and sucked her neck, making her tense up, then let out a deeper sound of arousal. Her back arched like a cat on defense. Rambo licked her breasts, kissed her small stomach like he was scared, as if the weight of the robbery was still hanging over him. He traced his damp mouth over her sensitive stomach, fueling her arousal, her wickedness. His eyes searched for her satisfaction before he slipped his tongue inside her navel, moving it as if he were trying to break into her body. That faux penetration excited her, made her wetter with anticipation, and then he moved his tongue over her thick thighs, sucking her inner thighs and then her pussy, opening her up with it.

Rambo unlocked her body with his tongue. With his fingers, he parted her walls, then used his tongue to paint her pussy, slipping it inside her, then sucking her clit like there was no tomorrow. Buffy's legs shook, her muscles tensed, and she took a deep breath, one that rose from her sacrum to her diaphragm. She felt like she was losing it. Buffy screamed out loud, but Rambo covered her mouth, trying, in vain, to silence her. He tongue-swiped her sex like he was licking the frosting off a cake.

Buffy moaned again, her body in waves. Rambo gave her a powerful lick, using the width of his tongue. He licked her the way she needed to be handled, hungry, almost ferocious. The greedy bastard devoured her, and seismic waves of pleasure ran through her body, tiny earthquakes that led to her orgasm. Buffy's sounds only encouraged him to torture her more. He dragged his tongue across her pussy, took a mouthful of her, sucked, and applied just enough pressure to wake up every nerve in her body. She quivered, cooed, and held his bald head.

Without embarrassment, he sucked her like a popsicle, making her back arch. As she swallowed a dozen heated moans, he ate her up, making slurping sounds. Glancing up at her, she smiled down at him. His tongue darted in and out, made circles, then plunged deep inside her pussy again. Buffy lost herself to the feeling.

Rambo stopped and whispered, "You're beautiful to me."

Buffy shook and gasped. "Your head game… stop talking in my ear and use your mouth," she said.

"What you want me to do with this mouth?" Rambo asked.

"You know what I want, so stop bullshitting and eat this pussy," Buffy replied.

"Tell me more, baby!" Rambo said.

"Suck and lick my pussy the way you sucked my tongue in the parking lot at *Club Thunder*," Buffy responded.

Rambo turned Buffy over, made her raise her ass, and put her in a crazy position. She bent over on all fours, her spine arched in a passive position. He didn't know what he was going to do next or which part of her body his long tongue would find as open for service. The position didn't matter; when they were younger, the position mattered to Buffy, he thought to himself.

Rambo's long fingers parted her pussy lips, exposing her to his breath, a long stream of air blown across her folds. Rambo blew and blew, then painted his name on her sex. Buffy eased down onto her shoulders, reached back, and spread her ass cheeks, showing Rambo what he wanted to see.

Rambo licked her sex with trills, rolling his wicked tongue in a vicious way, like a hood war out of control at a local mall center. Buffy's heart rate elevated, and the sounds of her pleasure filled the air.

It was fanatical, heated, and lovely. The nine hard muscles of Rambo's tongue were strong, like he did a thousand tongue push-ups every night—and more in the daytime. He inserted his tongue and gave her its full length. Buffy felt like a beautiful queen out of control. That long tongue was playing a game that switched her mind and body. Rambo played with her, changing the shape of his tongue, shortening it, lengthening it, flattening it out, licking her along her sex. Buffy couldn't take it anymore; she lost the ability to speak, could only breathe and swallow.

The sounds he made while eating her pussy blew her mind. His tongue flitted in and out of her, moving with the speed of a hummingbird. Buffy grabbed the bed sheets and became the bird that hummed. It was light and swift, the way he darted, the masterful way he fluttered and trilled. She couldn't stand it. Rambo's long tongue was the bee on honey, wide open. Nerves danced, and it ached so good—an itch and sweet irritation that magnified. Buffy started having orgasms, begging for Rambo to stop.

"Damn, little mama, you is literally dripping wet right now," Rambo said, lining the head of his dick with her hole, then stuffing it in her tight pussy. Buffy bit her bottom lip and moaned sexy sounds.

"Oh shit, mmmm, damn you in this pussy . . . I've been waiting on this special moment for a while," Buffy said.

"Take this dick and shut the fuck up, bitch!" Rambo said. He grabbed Buffy by her neck and pulled her into him, slamming his dick into her with all his man power.

"Hmmm-a, hummm-a . . . I can't, I can't take it, Rambo. You killing my pussy, baby. Oh shit! I'm cuming on this big dick . . . your bitch is cumming all over this dick. Ahh shit!" Buffy screamed.

Rambo could feel her pussy clamping down on his dick as she squirted all over the bed. Damn, that's gonna leave a mess on the sheets. Rambo pulled out, sat on the bed, and told Buffy to ride his dick until he came in her stomach. Buffy walked over to him, turned around, grabbed him, and laid him into her wet pussy. She rode him up and down, squeezing her pussy muscles on his dick as Rambo massaged and rubbed her ass cheeks, his big thumb sliding into her asshole. Rambo could feel his big nuts getting tight, and that's when he pushed his dick all the way in and let his seeds spill into her wet pussy.

"Let's go get in the shower and clean up real fast. Right now, we're sweaty as hell, and I feel nasty after fucking you," Buffy said.

"Don't put all the blame on me. You played a huge part in this shit too," Rambo replied. They gathered some clothes and headed to the shower together. Once in the shower, Rambo watched the hot water beat down on Buffy's nice titties, her pink nipples looking good. Rambo started feeling his manhood getting harder by the second, but he had to shower quick and handle some business. He left Buffy in the shower once he was finished. Rambo dried off, put on his clothes, and went into the bedroom to grab his backpack from the closet to hide the money away.

Buffy screamed from the bathroom." Rambo, where are you?

Rambo acted like he didn't hear Buffy scream. He dumped everything out of the backpack onto the bed and separated the money and dope he had stashed inside. From under the bed, he pulled out a brick of uncut heroin, another brick already broken down into zips, and a little over a half brick bagged up in $20 baggies and grams. Plus, Rambo still had the cocaine on lock around the hood. He put the dope back in the closet and started counting the money.

Once done, he counted $47,000. He pulled out $2,100.

Buffy walked into the bedroom, and her eyes got huge— damn near popped out of her head. "What's the business, Rambo?" she asked.

"Not shit," he replied.

"You putting my life in danger more and more each day. Where the fuck you get all that dope from?" Buffy asked, eyeing the clear plastic bags in the closet from a distance. "Is there anybody looking for that dope? We just did a robbery, so where all this extra money come from?"

"Baby, calm the fuck down. This money is ours. I need you to grab some food from the local store around the corner.

Get whatever you want. My keys on the kitchen table. Make sure you careful in my Benz," Rambo said.

"Okay, babe. I'll be back in a few," Buffy said.

Buffy walking out the front door made Rambo's day—he could finally handle what he was trying to do before she walked in. He couldn't believe how fast she got dressed, fresh out the shower and into the bedroom.

Rambo walked over to the nightstand, opened the bottom drawer, and grabbed some fresh rubber bands. He sat down and wrapped each stack up individually. He was taking $2,100 with him but wanted to make sure his stacks were straight first. He stopped and grabbed his phone, texting Tubb to see what was up:

Hey Tubb, I need you bad as fuck. I'm willing to shoot you an extra stack just for making that happen.

Rambo never mentioned what he needed in the text.

Tubb replied: *I can meet up with you in about two hours on the eastside, same spot like always. I got your whole order, plus more.*

Rambo: *What you want for everything?*

Tubb: *Give me $4,500, and I'll bless you with bullets for all the sticks, plus 100-round clips. Ima also throw in 32-round clips for all your Glocks.*

Rambo: *Okay, bet, my dude. Ima be at the spot in two hours with your money. There's a dirt road out back we can use to test them out. See you in a few.*

Suddenly, there was a hard knock at the front door. Rambo looked through the window and saw Buffy holding a bag in her hand. He opened the door and grabbed the bag from her.

Buffy walked in and took a seat on the couch. Rambo opened the bag, grabbed something to eat, and just as he started eating, his cell phone rang.

"Damn, who the fuck is this?" Rambo said, answering. "Hello?"

"Nigga, I'm about to ring some heat your way, 'cause word out you and Buffy killed my daughter," said a deep, threatening voice on the other end. It was Bambi.

"Wat da fuck you talkin' 'bout?" Rambo asked, his mind racing

This was exactly why he kept so many guns on deck— situations like this.

The call got disconnected after about twenty minutes.

Before Rambo could process what happened, Tubb pulled up outside the crib way earlier than expected. Turns out, he was already in traffic when they were texting but didn't say shit.

Tubb grabbed his phone and sent a quick text: *I'm outside.*

Rambo headed out to meet him, a grin spreading across his face when he saw his boy. Tubb hopped out of the car, walked to the trunk, and pulled out three large duffle bags.

"Come on, let's go inside the house," Rambo said.

He grabbed one of the duffle bags while Tubb took the other two. Once inside, Rambo locked the front door, then double-checked that the back door was locked, too. They went into the bedroom, but Buffy had disappeared from the couch. Rambo figured she was in the bedroom.

Tubb dumped the bags onto the bed and unzipped them. The first bag held an AR-15, five AK-47s, two Mini Dracos, and three SKs.

"You got ten sticks here. Everything comes with 100-round drums, except the ARs. Here go 50 boxes of shells for the AKs and SKs, and 10 boxes for the ARs. Now, in this other bag, I got all types of shit—two .40 Glocks, four .45 Colt 1911s, two Smith & Wessons. I'm also waiting on some Uzis to come in. If you want them, let me know," Tubb said.

"Nigga, I need everything you got. I'll take 'em off your hands—just put together a package for me and let me know the ticket," Rambo said.

"I got you, player," Tubb replied.

"Here go the money for all this shit," Rambo said, handing him the stacks.

Tubb took the cash and walked out the bedroom, heading straight to his car without counting it. Something felt off, but he didn't say a word.

"Damn, I got enough shit to set this hood war off. I pray Bambi stay in her lane. 'Cause if she don't, she gon' be a dead bitch," Rambo muttered.

Tubb had Bambi waiting around the corner at a local store. He pulled up and picked her up.

She got in the car with a smile.

On the way to the trap house, Bambi made sure to handle Tubb. She rubbed his dick through his jeans, teasing him the whole ride. By the time they got inside the house, she was on her knees.

Bambi pulled Tubb's dick out and started eating it up like it was her last meal. She breathed on the tip before taking him in her mouth. She licked the head like a lollipop, then swallowed him whole, sucking loudly while moaning all around him. The heat from her mouth had Tubb's toes curling.

He reached over her shoulders and grabbed her big booty, pulling up her Baby Phat skirt to expose her bare pussy. He slid two fingers inside her wetness, fingering her fast and deep. The faster he went, the faster she sucked his dick.

His eyes rolled back as he lost himself in the sensation.

When he opened them again, her breasts were bouncing together, and that sight made him thrust his fingers even harder inside her. He started humping into her mouth, hitting the back of her throat.

Bambi pulled his dick out, licked the head, and rubbed it all over her face before deep-throating him again.

That was all it took. His stomach tightened, his nuts tensed as he felt his cum rising in his nut sacks, and then he exploded, letting it all fly into her mouth.

"Mmm . . . mmm . . . mmm…" was all Bambi could say, her lips still wrapped around his dick, milking him.

A wicked smile crossed her face.

"Baby, I want them niggas dead that killed my daughter," Bambi said.

"It's gonna happen. Just chill, baby," Tubb replied.

"Okay," she whispered.

They held each other, then laid down for the night.

Chapter 9

Two days later, Bambi parked her car in the cut, close enough to see Rambo when he made it home. Hours passed, and still no sign of him. She was about ready to give up when Tubb suddenly shouted, "There he go right there!"

Tubb whispered, "Let's handle this bitch."

They pulled their masks over their faces, slipped on black gloves, and checked their handguns to make sure they were fully loaded. Moving in silence, they walked up to the entrance. Rambo's crib had a security gate, which pissed Bambi off—until she spotted a man walking up.

Thinking quick, Bambi started a conversation with the man, making him feel wanted. She flirted just enough to lower his guard, and soon enough, he let her through the gate. Once she was in, Bambi slipped away from him and knocked on the front door.

"Yes? Who is it?" a voice called from inside.

"You got an order from Amazon," Bambi said smoothly.

Tubb eased up right behind her.

Rambo frowned inside. "I ain't order shit . . . unless Buffy ordered some shoes," he muttered, opening the door.

The second that door cracked open, Bambi rushed in with her handgun raised, making sure Rambo couldn't make a move. Tubb was right beside her, silent but ready for war.

"Bet you ain't think you'd see me again, huh?" Bambi said.

Tubb laughed, then cracked Rambo across the head with the bottom of his handgun. Blood immediately started running down Rambo's face.

"I suggest you put the gun down and get the fuck outta here before you regret this," Rambo growled, blood dripping down onto his shirt.

Boom! Boom! Boom!

Tubb fired off three shots. "I won't do what? Say it again, bitch! Now who the bitch?" Tubb snarled.

Rambo gritted his teeth. "The fuck y'all want? Money? I got plenty of it in the closet."

Bambi stepped up. "Get your bitch ass up and go get the money before I murder you right now!" she snapped.

Rambo, now bleeding from a fresh bullet wound in his right leg, crawled toward the bedroom, dragging himself toward the closet. He stumbled up to his feet, threw the safe open fast as hell, then spun around and let off a shot at Tubb's head.

He missed.

Bambi rushed in and let off four shots.

Boom! Boom! Boom! Boom!

Three bullets hit the wall.

The fourth one hit Rambo dead in the chest.

Rambo flew back against the wall, blood pouring from the wound. He was still breathing, struggling, crawling toward his .40 Glock.

Bambi cocked her head. "Where the fuck you think you goin'?" She spit on the floor. "Stupid bitch, this about my daughter Jade. The one you killed. Revenge, motherfucker."

Boom!

Bambi and Tubb rushed into the kitchen, grabbed a large garbage bag, and filled it with money from the safe. Once done, they slipped out the front door, looking around to make sure Buffy wasn't nearby.

Tubb popped the trunk and threw the bag inside. They jumped in the car, creeping slowly past the security guards at the gate, then headed to Rambo's second crib on the westside.

Buffy's Location – Westside

Buffy was on the westside at Rambo's other crib, deep in a quiet neighborhood. Any loud noise would wake the neighbors. The lights were off, but inside, Buffy was moving around, searching through the room.

Maybe she was looking for weapons, money, or dope.

Tubb, the lockpicking expert, had them there in no time.

When he was younger, his big brother used to lock him in the closet, forcing him to pick his way out. That practice made him a pro.

"Check your straps and remember where the fuck we at. This spot got hella cops around," Tubb warned as they pulled up.

They moved fast.

They entered through the back door into the kitchen.

The music inside was blasting.

Buffy had no idea what was coming.

They had to move quick—not giving her time to grab her gun or react to the ambush.

Tubb barked as Buffy tried to creep to her gun, "You too slow, bitch!"

Buffy snapped her head up, eyes wild. "The fuck y'all want? Get it and leave me the fuck alone!"

Bambi's voice rang through the house. "We came for one thing!"

"What's that?" Buffy asked.

Bambi grinned. "Your life, bitch."

Buffy narrowed her eyes. "Bitch, y'all crazy. You really think you gon' kill me and get away with it?"

Bambi noddded, laughing hysterically.

Boom! Boom!

Buffy's body dropped.

Tubb and Bambi rushed through the house, flipping shit over, searching.

They stumbled across a few stacks of money hidden under the bed in another room—stuffed in a red shoebox.

Four shoeboxes full.

They snatched everything, then rushed out, leaving Buffy shot on the floor, the music still blasting.

Once outside, Tubb and Bambi jumped into the car, pulling off smooth.

They headed back to the eastside, finding a spot to dump the evidence and the whip.

Tubb poured gas all over the car, then tossed in their masks and gloves.

Then he struck a match.

Flames erupted.

No witnesses.

No evidence.

No loose ends.

"Hold up," Bambi said, taking off her mask and gloves and tossing them into the fire.

Hearing police sirens in the distance, they jumped into another car and hit the nearest freeway.

Tubb had a motel room reserved in Gosnell, Arkansas, for months. Behind them, the car and everything in it blazed like hell.

"That shit felt good!" Bambi shouted.

Tubb nodded. "These bitch-ass niggas killed Jade."

"How much money we get?" Bambi interrupted.

"Between the two, we came up on 170 stacks—that's 85 apiece," Tubb replied.

He assumed that was the correct amount after running it through the small money counter in their car.

After changing their clothes, Bambi ordered takeout. They sat back in the motel room, watching the local news. The car had been discovered, but there was no mention of Rambo or Buffy being killed.

A few hours passed. Feeling like the coast was clear, they sat back, reflecting on the situation.

"How long you think it'll be before they find 'em?" Bambi asked.

"Really don't fucking care at this point," Tubb replied.

Tubb was exhausted. He gathered some clothes and went to take a shower. He had been staying at the motel so long, it felt like home, with all his shit laid out everywhere.

He stayed in the shower for about twenty minutes, then came out to see what Bambi was doing.

She was lying in bed, legs wide open, playing with herself.

"You like what you see, Tubb?" Bambi asked, teasing him.

"Hell yeah, baby. You got a nice bald-head pussy. Come here to Daddy," Tubb instructed.

"This your time to punish me. You earned this, baby. Let me take off that towel," Bambi said.

She pulled the towel from around Tubb's waist and laid him back on the bed. The second she touched him, his dick stood at attention.

Bambi traced his muscular body with warm Gucci oil, giving him a deep, sensual massage. The oil started to heat up, making his skin tingle.

She popped a peppermint in her mouth, then slowly eased the head of his dick past her lips.

"Damn, Bambi, that shit feel so damn good," Tubb moaned.

"You like having this big dick in my throat?" Bambi asked, looking up at him.

"Yes, honey, suck this big dick! It's yours," Tubb groaned.

She kept sucking, her tongue swirling around the head, her lips sliding up and down his length until he was on the edge of cumming.

Right before he busted, she pulled him out and blew softly on the tip.

Tubb's whole body locked up.

Seconds later, he started nutting, but before he could react, Bambi eased his dick back into her mouth.

His body jerked, trying to escape, but Bambi snatched him closer.

The combination of the peppermint and her throat game had him rolling all over the bed, trying to get away.

"Damn, baby, a nigga never came like this before! You mine forever now," Tubb groaned, catching his breath.

He thought he was done. Thought the night was over.

Bambi had other plans.

She climbed on top of his face, and like a homeless man who hadn't eaten in days, Tubb dove into her pussy with his tongue.

"Slow down, nigga, and enjoy eating this pussy," she moaned, grinding against his face.

"That's it. That's how I like it. We ain't in no rush."

Bambi smirked down at him.

"It's yours, big daddy. Make this pussy cum in your mouth."

Tubb did exactly what she told him.

He slowed down, savoring every taste, flicking his tongue against her clit, sucking her lips, dragging his tongue deep inside her.

Bambi shivered, then flipped around, sliding into a 69 position, bringing his dick back to life.

After a while, she climbed off his face and rolled a pink condom onto his dick with her wet mouth.

Then she eased him inside her—slow, deep.

Tubb groaned as she started grinding against him, rolling her hips, milking his dick.

He smacked her thick ass cheeks, making her bounce harder.

Bambi rode him like a pro, taking every inch, her pussy gripping him like a vice.

"Baby, I love you so much. This some good pussy and head you got."

Tubb groaned.

"Damn, this pussy off the chain!"

Thinking about everything they had just done—the revenge, the money, the sex, the power—they both busted a nut at the same time.

Exhausted, they held each other close, bodies tangled together.

Within minutes, they passed out, knocked out cold.

Chapter 10

Coca pulled up to the trap house, her tight-ass shorts riding up her curves. As soon as she hopped out of her 2024 Benz, the niggas in the hood started trying their luck, calling out to get her attention.

Coca had the kind of beauty that didn't need enhancements. Gucci liked her just like that—he wasn't into all that makeup shit women wore.

But one thing Coca wasn't giving up was her red and blue hair. She loved her some Gucci, but cutting off her weave wasn't happening. Not now, not ever.

Since summer was right around the corner, Coca had switched up her style, rocking a new yellow-blonde color that flowed down her back.

Gucci stood outside, watching Coca walk across the yard with a bag in her hand.

"C'mere for a minute," he called out.

Coca cut her eyes at him and thought, *I can't believe this crazy-ass nigga still around bullshitting.*

"Baby, you look amazing in them tight-ass shorts. What you got for Big Daddy in that bag?" Gucci asked.

"Not shit for your thirsty ass, nigga." Coca smirked.

Gucci screwed up his face at her reaction, feeling some type of way. He couldn't believe she was talking shit to him like that.

She walked past him, headed toward the house.

"Gucci, open the back door for me," Coca said.

Gucci unlocked the front door instead, letting her in. Coca stepped inside and set the bag down on the nearest table.

She made her way into the kitchen to unpack the little bit of food she had.

Gucci strolled up behind her, wrapping his arms around her small waist. He kissed her softly on the jaw.

"What you doing with these little-ass shorts on?" Gucci asked.

Coca's pussy was soaked just from his touch.

She cooed, "These old things? You like them, huh?"

"Hell yeah. Let me see what this shit be like," Gucci whispered in her ear as he unbuttoned her shorts and slid his hand down her pants.

Coca tried to act like she wasn't into it, pretending to be more worried about their food getting cold.

"Babe, that can wait. I don't want our food to get cold," she said, trying to resist.

"Be quiet and enjoy the moment. You don't like it?" Gucci asked.

"Hell naw, nigga!" Coca gasped.

Gucci chuckled. "You a damn lie. This pussy soaking wet for a nigga right now."

He pulled her shorts all the way down to the floor.

His dick was already hard as a rock.

When he realized she wasn't wearing any panties, that shit turned him on even more.

Gucci was only wearing some gym shorts. He slid them off quick, then glided his dick across her ass cheeks.

Coca knew what time it was.

She bent over the table and grabbed his dick with her left hand, stroking him.

"See how much Larry been missing this good pussy?" Gucci murmured.

Coca moaned softly.

"Stop playing and make this pussy call your name, Gucci," she demanded.

As Gucci pushed inside her, she let out a sharp gasp—like his dick just gave her life again.

Every time Gucci fucked Coca or had her sucking his dick, he made sure to punish her pussy.

Coca hollered like a bitch.

"Cum in this good pussy, young player," she moaned, throwing her pussy back at him.

They had to hurry before somebody walked in and ruined their session.

Coca started squeezing her pussy muscles around his dick, making that shit grip him. Then, with her free hand, she played with her clit.

Shit had been so stressful with the cartel; it was putting a dent in their relationship. They barely saw each other anymore unless it was at the trap spot or a club in the hood.

Coca dropped to her knees.

She trailed kisses up Gucci's chest, to his neck, then to his ear.

Gucci let out a soft moan like a bitch.

Just from her touch, his dick was rock hard again.

She stroked him slowly as she kissed along his muscular body.

Then, she started making small kisses on his large dick, teasing him.

Coca took her time, sliding him into her mouth, inch by inch, while she continued stroking.

Gucci had a huge-ass dick—twelve inches long, black, and thick. Just looking at it could make a bitch horny.

As she bobbed up and down, Coca's pussy got even wetter.

Gucci tilted his head back, groaning. Her warm mouth wrapped around his prized possession.

Coca was sucking the shit outta Gucci's dick.

"You like this?" Coca asked, looking up at him.

"Hell yeah! Ah, fuck—I'm 'bout to cum, baby!" Gucci groaned.

"Cum for a bitch, baby," Coca whispered. On command, Gucci's body began to shake as his dick exploded like a bomb in Coca's mouth.

Like the bad bitch she was, she slurped up all his nut, swallowing every drop. Coca kept sucking, not letting go until his dick came back to life.

Then, she pulled out a condom, slid it down onto him with her wet mouth, and mounted his dick slowly. It was too big to just hop on like a chair. She moved up and down, letting her pussy adjust until she could finally take all of it. Once she did, she gave Gucci the ride of his life.

Gucci started moaning like a bitch, his hands smacking Coca's ass cheeks. Trying to hold back from cumming too fast, he suddenly stood up, turned her around, and bent her over—forcing her hands to wrap around her ankles.

Then he dove in.

Nice and slow.

Full force.

Coca damn near collapsed.

"Oh fuck! Beat this shit up!" she screamed.

Gucci grabbed her small arms, pinned them behind her back, and started beating her pussy up harder and harder.

By the fourth stroke, Coca was already losing it.

"Oh, bitch! Hell yeah! I'm cumming!"

"Take this dick, bitch!" Gucci growled, digging deeper, hitting all her walls.

He felt himself about to cum, but he wanted one more nut out of her first.

"Cum with Big Dick Daddy," Gucci demanded.

He let one of her arms go but kept fucking the dog shit out of her while he stroked her pearl tongue.

As his body began to shake, nutting hard as fuck, Coca came at the same time.

They collapsed on top of each other, completely out of breath.

Gucci grinned and sang in her ear, "It was the greatest sex I ever had from a Black woman."

They both broke out in laughter.

"You so crazy," Coca giggled.

Gucci grabbed her hand and led her into the shower.

Neither of them said a word—just bathed each other, dried off, and laid together.

But while they lay in each other's arms, their minds were in two different places.

Gucci was thinking Coca was the one.

Coca?

All she could think about was killing his ass.

Chapter 11

The next morning, they woke up, ate breakfast, and went their separate ways, promising to talk later that evening.

When Coca made it home, she knew something wasn't right.

Walking into the living room, she saw Eve sitting there quietly, watching TV.

Coca sat on the loveseat, turned on a basketball game, and ended up falling asleep.

She was snapped awake by Eve screaming in her ear.

Coca, still groggy, thought she'd heard wrong.

"You said what happened?" Coca asked, sitting up.

Eve shook her head, looking shook.

"Boss was found on the west side . . . Somebody cut off his dick and stuck it in his mouth."

Coca's eyes widened.

Eve continued, "They killed him for no reason 'cause he wasn't the one that got Rambo killed."

Coca froze, her mind racing.

Someone was coming for her cartel.

And whoever it was?

They had to be close.

"I can't see no man cutting off this nigga's dick," Coca admitted. "Maybe a bitch set him up at *Club Thunder*."

She stood up, grabbing her keys.

"I'ma hit a few blocks, see if the streets talkin'. Keep shit afloat and get ready for war."

She walked out the door and jumped into her Range Rover.

Coca headed to her crib on the east side.

When she pulled up, she scanned the area before stepping out.

Once inside, she rushed to the bedroom, stripping off her clothes and stepping into a hot shower.

The water relaxed her body, but her mind was racing.

She knew she had to move fast, or the streets would think she was a weak bitch.

And if it was a man behind Boss's murder?

She was ready for war, too.

After getting out the shower, Coca went into the closet, grabbed a large duffle bag, and filled it with cash and clothes.

Then she slipped on a fresh outfit.

It was time to pull up on Gucci and see what the word was.

Plus, it was a good excuse to spend more time with him.

She threw her duffle bag in the backseat of her 2024 Range Rover, then grabbed her phone and texted Gucci:

"On my way to you."

As she stopped at the red light at Ash and Maple, she sent a quick text to Tubb:

"Hey, baby! I'm sliding back your way, hope to see you soon. I'll call when I get close."

Minutes went by, and no reply.

Maybe he laid up with Bambi, she thought.

She kept driving.

Coca pulled onto Maple Street and immediately knew something was off.

Blunts of weed were blazing. Hennessy bottles passed around. Young bad bitches were posted up on older men like they was ready to start some shit.

The vibe wasn't right.

Coca decided not to risk it.

She needed somewhere lowkey.

Somewhere nobody would think to look for her.

She found a nice motel and checked in.

Once inside her motel room, she pulled out her phone.

Still no word from Tubb.

That nigga suspect as fuck right now.

Boss man was a man of God.

A father of three. He loved his kids with all his heart

Whoever set him up, Coca needed to find them fast.

She unpacked her belongings, tucked her money away, and strapped on her bullet-proof vest.

Then there was a hard knock at the door.

"Who is it?" Coca called out.

"It's me, Gucci, baby."

She unlocked the door, surprised.

As soon as she locked it back, she turned around—and Gucci was already on her.

His lips crashed into hers.

She wrapped her legs around him as he grabbed her ass and pinned her to the wall.

They kissed sloppy, deep.

Gucci had one hand gripping her round ass, the other tangled in her hair, pulling her head back so he could suck on her neck.

By the time he set her back down on her feet, a dark hickey was already forming around her neck.

Gucci just stood there, watching her.

She wasn't thin like his other bitches.

But Coca had enough meat on her to have fun with.

Coca sat on the chair, slipping off her shoes.

Then, slowly, she stood up, pulled down her dress.

The way that red fabric hugged her curves had Gucci's dick sprung up in his shorts.

Coca saw how excited Gucci was.

She grabbed him by the waist, pulled him in front of her, then dropped his shorts to his knees, taking his boxers off at the same time.

His dick stuck out, stiff as a flagpole, brushing against her lips.

She moaned.

Gucci felt the warm wetness of her mouth as she took the tip of his big dick inside.

"Damn, I ain't no white bitch. I can suck a white boy dick good," Coca teased with a smile.

Her mouth was wet as hell.

She called Gucci a white boy 'cause of his light skin, but his mom was Black and his daddy was white.

"Coca's head game nasty and sloppy as fuck . . . but damn, it's good." Gucci groaned.

Coca sucked hard and fast, using no hands, making his dick slam the back of her throat.

She gagged, tears rolling down her face, while her nose ran, all while massaging his big nuts.

Gucci couldn't take much more.

His nut shot into her mouth— hard, like a pro football player hitting the end zone for a touchdown.

Coca swallowed most of it, then let the rest drip from her lips onto her chest.

Smiling, she rubbed the cum on her breasts, then licked her tongue across them, tasting him.

Gucci pulled her up, turned her around, and smacked her thick ass hard.

First the left cheek.

Then the right.

Coca jumped and screamed out loud.

Gucci kept smacking, leaving red handprints on her ass.

Then he ripped off her red thong and bent her over the tall chair in the corner of the room.

"Damn, baby, you dripping wet right now."

Gucci lined the tip of his dick with her tight, hot, gushy pussy and slammed it in.

Coca bit her bottom lip, moaning sexy as fuck.

"Oh shit! Damn, you deep inside me . . . I can't get enough of this big dick!" Coca gasped.

"Shut the fuck up. Take this big dick."

Gucci grabbed her by the neck, pulling her into him, slamming his dick inside her with pure aggression.

"I can't . . . I can't take all this dick! Oh shit, baby! You beating my pussy up! I'm cumming all over this big dick!" Coca screamed.

"You my daddy for life with this big dick."

Gucci felt her pussy clamping down, gripping him tight as she squirted all over the chair.

Damn, that's gonna leave a big-ass mess, he thought.

Gucci pulled out, sat on the bed, and told Coca to ride his dick until he nutted.

Coca turned around, grabbed ahold of him, and slid his thick dick back into her hot, dripping pussy.

She rode him slow at first, then picked up the pace, squeezing her pussy muscles around him.

Gucci groaned, massaging and rubbing her ass, sliding his big thumb into her tight asshole.

He could feel his nutsack tightening up.

That's when he slammed his dick all the way in, letting his seed spill deep inside her.

Gucci pulled out, then slid his fingers into Coca's pussy while sucking on her nipples.

He could feel her wetness seeping past his fingers. The scent of her pussy drove him insane.

Gucci threw Coca's thighs over his shoulders, pulling her pussy to his mouth.

He peeled her pink lips apart, exposing her big clit, then sucked it into his mouth.

Loud slurping sounds filled the room.

His grip on her thick ass tightened as he slid a finger into her asshole.

Freaky nigga, Coca thought.

"Damn, you eating my pussy so good. Oh shit!" Coca screamed.

Gucci fingered her asshole harder, forcing her to hump against his face.

His tongue flicked against her clit, licking up and down her crease.

He tongue-fucked her tight, sweet-tasting pussy, sucking all over her pussylips, pulling on them with his mouth.

Coca sat up on his shoulders, rocking back and forth, gripping his hair.

"I'm 'bout to bust a nut all over your face, nigga."

Gucci gripped her ass harder, sucking and slurping faster until Coca exploded in his face.

Just as she came, they heard a loud banging at the front door.

"Who is it?" Gucci barked.

Boom! Boom! Boom!

Coca rushed to the door, wrapping a sheet around her body. Gucci stood behind her.

Coca was surprised to see Eve's face when she opened the door. She kissed Eve on her lips, her heart beating like a drumline at a football game.

Gucci eased back in the house, out of sight. Eve didn't even notice him standing behind Coca.

"Bitch, I bet those bags are heavy." Coca grabbed the duffle bags from Eve and walked inside the house. Eve followed, smiling.

Once they sat next to each other on the couch, Eve instructed Coca to look inside the duffle bags. Coca reached down and opened the first duffle bag.

Coca couldn't believe her eyes.

A shitload of cocaine.

She also saw some weed. Coca grabbed the weed and counted seven pounds what looked like Cali plug shit.

"I'm about to really flood the streets with this shit," Coca said, stuffing ten bricks of coke into a smaller duffle.

She unzipped the second bag—

Guns.

"Damn."

She slid the duffle bag under the bed.

Coca suddenly realized . . .

Where the fuck was Gucci?

She checked the bathroom, under the bed—nothing. She returned to the living room.

"Follow me to my car. I got a bag for you to hold down until I get back," Eve said.

Coca followed Eve outside to her truck.

Eve opened the back door, reached inside, and handed Coca twelve thousand in cash.

"This'll hold you till I get back," Eve said.

Coca kissed her on the lips.

"Thank you, Eve. Call me when you get there."

"Baby, I love you. You my everything," Eve said, acting like Sexxy Red.

Coca laughed. "Love you too."

Eve made a quick stop at a local store to grab something to eat.

She reached inside her purse, grabbed her phone, and called Coca.

Line busy.

She tried again.

Coca finally answered.

"Hello?"

"What's up?" Eve asked.

"Girl, I fell asleep that fast."

She was lying. Gucci was right beside her in bed.

"Lemme take a quick shower, I'ma call you right back."

"Okay." Eve checked the duffle bags in her backseat, making sure nothing had been fucked with.

She got out and walked toward the store—

Then—

A black Chevy Caprice skidded to a stop in the middle of the street.

Windows rolled down.

40 rounds let off.

Eve dove behind a blue Range Rover.

Just as she pulled her Glock, ready to fire back—

The car sped off.

She had to get the fuck outta there before the cops pulled up.

With a car full of drugs and guns, she wasn't about to get caught up like her homies Bank Roll and LA.

Eve hopped back in the vehicle and sped over the bridge, headed to a safe spot where she could get this dope off her.

She took all the back roads home, trying to avoid the laws and anyone who might have been following her.

After making sure she wasn't being tailed, she pulled into her driveway and exited the vehicle.

She punched in the code on her keypad to open the garage door, parked inside, and let the door down behind her.

Grabbing the duffle bag from the backseat, she headed inside.

She went straight to the bedroom, dumped the duffle bags on the bed, and sorted through everything.

Once she saw everything was there, she put it away, then went to take a shower.

The hot water ran down her shoulders, but all she could think about was—

Who the fuck just tried to take her life?

Could've been someone hating on her for being with Gucci—a mixed-race nigga but with a Black soul.

Damn.

Eve thought she had the streets figured out, but she was wrong.

Somebody's gonna pay for Boss's death . . . and for shooting at me.

She washed up, dried off, then walked into the bedroom, lotioned up, and put on some clothes for the night.

She climbed into bed and knocked out fast.

But before she knew it—

Her phone started ringing.

Eve blinked awake, confused.

She looked at her phone several times as a message popped up, catching her attention.

She reached into her purse, grabbed her weed, and rolled up a blunt as she jumped out of bed, pacing the room.

Lighting the blunt, she shook her head, side to side.

Then she grabbed her second phone, checked the screen, and read the text:

"Boss was beefing with another gang on the west side. His trap house got robbed, and everybody in there got flatlined. They killed him because the gang said they couldn't catch up with you, Eve."

This shit started coming back to Eve's mind again.

Eve dropped her phone in disbelief at what she just read in the text message.

She threw her blunt down, picked up her phone, and walked inside the house.

Eve grabbed her duffle bags from the closet and was on her way back out the front door.

She stopped, unzipped one of the duffle bags, grabbed four stacks, then walked out into the garage. She got into her car and left.

Thirty minutes later, Eve pulled up to her secret hideout.

A suspicious-looking car was parked a few houses down, so she didn't pull into the driveway.

Eve rode past them, trying to get a better look.

She grabbed her cell phone and tried to call Gucci, but nobody answered.

Eve saw another car on the block and thought it was Gucci—but it wasn't.

She parked around the block, then walked up on them to see what they were up to.

But something in her gut told her—

It's them.

The same motherfuckers that shot at her last time.

Eve grabbed her Glock and hit the cut, but by the time she got back on the main block, the car was gone.

"I'ma murk a bitch tonight."

Eve went back, got in the car, and hit a few blocks again to see if she could find the car, but it was nowhere to be found.

She pulled up to the duck-off, reversed, and parked.

Then she went inside, grabbed the rest of her dope.

Her phone started ringing.

"Hello?" Eve said.

"Bitch, we need to get to the bottom of this real soon before somebody gets killed."

Tubb had jumped ship on her crew, now he was calling her.

"Nigga, I knew you couldn't be trusted, and I gave you a chance like the rest of these niggas. It's war between us now. Fuck you and the crew you with, bitch!" Eve snapped.

"I will continue to kill everything you love—even your dog-ass mama on the east side of town, bitch!" Tubb said.

A female voice cut in.

"Hold up, who that bitch talking all that shit like she cut like that, Tubb?"

"It's that bitch Eve, the one who gonna wish she never spoke to a nigga like me," Tubb said.

"Well, let's get ready for war, 'cause Eve got a nice goon squad on the east side. The bitch think she the only one who can take down a cartel with a bloody war. She 'bout to see the real thug town— bitch, we kill for a hobby, no matter the situation." Boon said.

"Chill the fuck out, baby. We gon' handle this shit!" Tubb said.

"Nawl, this bitch got the game fucked up." Boon hit the blunt, coughed, and gave Tubb a mean look. "That bitch mine. I'm the devil's child . . . and she the prey that's about to be dead along with her family."

Boon paced back and forth through the house.

She knew it was about to go down.

Tubb's phone buzzed.

"Hold up . . . who the fuck is texting me like crazy?" Tubb said.

He glanced at the screen.

A text from Eve.

"Nigga, meet me on the east side at the park tomorrow. Bring your whole crew, including your mama." Eve put a smiley face at the end of the text.

Tubb read the message out loud.

"Baby, you see what this bitch just texted me?"

Boon leaned over his shoulder, read it, then rolled her eyes.

"That bitch crazy. We gon' handle her—period. No more talking, no more texting.

She might be the plug with the feds.

You know bitches will try to get you off the streets quick."

Tubb nodded.

"You right, Boon, baby."

He put his phone down.

Tomorrow, shit was about to get real.

Chapter 12

Thirty minutes later, Eve went to the north side to pick up Coca. As they rode, Eve explained everything to Coca from start to finish. Gucci sat there, listening to the whole conversation without saying a damn word.

"Now, Coca, we need to get all the weapons we need for this war. That bitch Boon is the main leader of their cartel," Eve said.

She dumped her duffle bag out on the floor, revealing the arsenal inside—a .45 automatic handgun, a .32 handgun, three 9mm handguns, four grenades, three .40 Glock handguns, and a broken-down AR-15 with an extra sixty-round clip.

"Damn, bitch, you mean business right now," Coca said with a smile.

"It's war time. Pick out what you want. We taking all these weapons," Eve replied.

"I'm ready."

Gucci sat back, chilling with his hand on his .40 Glock.

He had the straight face of a killer—like Charles Manson, ready to take a life at any moment.

The three of them headed to the block together.

Eve grabbed her cell phone and dialed Tubb's number.

After three rings, Tubb picked up.

"Hello."

"Nigga, meet me on West Rose. Bring your whole crew, 'cause you gon' need them."

Eve smiled to herself.

"Fuck you, bitch. I'm a soldier—I go to war by myself." Tubb shot back.

Boon's voice cut in.

"Baby, that's that bitch Eve talking shit again? We 'bout to show her we mean business. She know we own this town, not them."

Eve hung up, smirking.

She drove through the streets with Coca and Gucci, all of them locked and loaded, heading to the block for war.

All three had their hands on their guns, ready to handle business at any moment.

Eve pulled up to the scene.

Several young niggas were standing around.

The second Eve's crew stepped out the car, people started running—

But for some, it was too damn late.

Eve raised her .40 Glock first and let that bitch spit.

Coca followed, blasting her 9mm.

Then Gucci opened fire with his AR-15.

The block erupted.

Bam! Bam! Bam!

Gunfire ripped through the air like a bomb went off in the middle of a football field.

Men and women screamed.

Blood splattered everywhere.

People tried to take cover, but some got hit in the legs, backs, and arms before they could make it to safety.

Eve walked up on Tubb, who had been shot trying to get away.

She stood over him, aimed, and put three bullets in his head.

Then Coca walked up on Boon.

"Now, bitch, you had all that mouth on the phone."

Boon held her leg, blood oozing between her fingers.

"Please, don't hurt me. I'll help you find the rest of the cartel," Boon pleaded, her voice shaking.

"Bitch, get up. You coming with us," Coca snapped.

Gucci glared at her.

"Bitch, we told you what was gon' happen," Gucci said.

They snatched Boon up, dragged her into the car, and pressed her for information.

"Where the rest of your crew at?"

"I'll show you. Make a right at that corner house," Boon mumbled, wincing in pain.

Eve pulled right up in front of a blue house.

She laid on the horn—long and loud.

Out of nowhere, a masked person ran out the front yard, gripping a handgun.

Boom! Boom! Boom!

"Damn, I can't believe I'm hit . . ." the masked person gasped, stumbling.

Coca sprayed up the trap house, emptying her clip.

Then they peeled off, burning rubber down the street.

They tossed Boon out the car, her body hitting the pavement with a hard thud.

Before speeding off, Eve yelled—

"Tell that bitch Bambi we'll be back for her!"

Boon groaned in pain, barely able to lift her head.

"Okay," she mumbled.

Many hours later, Gucci brought in more heavy artillery.

They had plenty of AR-15 assault rifles, handguns, bulletproof vests, RPGs, and even silencers.

Eve grabbed an AR-15, smiling. "It's war time, baby," she said, then shot in the air.

"We need an old bucket for this next mission," Coca said.

"I got some young white boys who keep stolen cars in their backyards. I just give them some dope and money whenever I need one. They stay in my corner," Gucci said.

"Bitch, I'm ready for war," Eve said.

"I just texted one of the young niggas on Maple Street to meet me at the same spot we been doing business," Gucci added.

They hit the block a few more times, then pulled up and waited for the young niggas to bring the stolen car.

***

The Ambush

Bambi was getting ready to strike.

"We about to walk up and hit these bitches on their block at close range," one of her goons said.

One of their targets tried to run, but Bambi was too fast.

Boom! Boom! Boom! Boom!

Shots rang out.

Gucci took four bullets to the chest, dropping face-first into the pavement.

A rain of gunfire followed. One of the shooters that shot Gucci cleaned up behind himself. Then the house door swung open, and more shots came flying from the side window and front door.

Coca took cover behind a truck, but she could see more people letting off shots at the house.

She grabbed Eve, and they ran behind the house, diving under the bed in the bedroom for safety.

Outside, the gunfire was nonstop.

Boom! Boom! Boom!

Coca heard shots getting closer to the bedroom.

She eased out from under the bed and started firing out the side window.

Coca was shooting like she was in a war movie.

Then, suddenly—

Eve slid out from under the bed and joined in, firing out the window.

Each of them emptied about twenty rounds from their handguns, spraying at Bambi and her crew.

Meanwhile, Gucci was dead outside, his body motionless on the ground.

"Ahh shit, bitch! I got shot in the chest," Eve groaned.

Her chest felt like it was on fire.

She walked into the front room, spotting a Mexican man dead on the floor, an AR-15 still clutched in his hands.

Eve eased out the front door, trying to see if the shooters had left.

The gunfire had calmed down.

She made it a few more yards and then saw Gucci's lifeless body.

"Oh shit!" Eve screamed.

Coca heard the scream and jumped out the side window to check on her bitch.

She thought Eve had been hit bad, but when she saw her up close—

It was the bulletproof vest that saved her. The impact probably left a mark on her chest, but she was okay.

Coca's eyes filled with tears as she looked at Gucci's dead body.

"We gotta get outta here now, 'cause I'm almost out of bullets, Eve," Coca said.

Both of them kissed Gucci on the forehead, then jumped in their car and sped off from the scene.

***

"Damn, Bambi, them hoes got away again," Marco said.

"At least we murdered one of their crew members. Maybe two."

Marco shook his head.

"In this shit, somebody gotta die. You know a nigga is down for you.

This shit crazy—these hoes out here fucking a white man for a bag of money."

Bambi and Marco eased out of an old house across the street, hopped into their car, and left the scene.

"This shit funny to me," Marco said as he let off several rounds from his AR-15 out the car window.

He was tripping—nobody was even around.

"These bitches belong to me now. I'm the fucking devil," Marco said, smirking at Bambi.

Bambi laughed.

"Marco, let's go get cleaned up. I wanna give you some of this good pussy and fire head."

As they drove off, a black SUV with dark-tinted windows sat parked in the cut.

They didn't notice.

They kept driving toward their house, ready to relax.

***

Coca and Eve had switched cars. They sat inside a dark SUV, watching Marco and Bambi pass by.

Bambi kept driving back and forth, trying to see inside.

The SUV looked like an unmarked Feds vehicle, sitting low in the cut.

"Damn, Bambi, I wonder who that is in that Range Rover?" Marco asked.

"Nigga, stop trippin'. That's probably just a trick getting his dick sucked by a crackhead for some money or dope," Bambi said.

"Shit, I wish that was me getting some fire head right now," Marco said.

***

Coca and Eve arrived at their safe spot on the northside of town—where all the white folks lived.

Before stepping out, they looked around, making sure nobody was watching.

"Bitch, hurry up with your scary ass. You should be a goon after all that dick you been taking lately from the strap-on I been punishing you with," Coca teased.

She grabbed Eve's round ass and kissed her lips.

Coca dug inside her Chanel purse, looking for her house key.

Once she found it, she unlocked the door.

Eve rushed inside, kicked off her heels, and sat down.

"Baby, I was just playin' about you takin' all that strap-on inside your tight pussy. But you do be holding it down when we fucking strong," Coca said.

Eve laughed.

"Right now, shit crazy out here. We two women in love, and these streets ain't never gon' understand it. Bambi gotta die soon."

"True to that, love. We been holding it down a long time. Shit about to change—fast. No matter who likes it or not."

Coca smirked. "I know you had a long night on the block. Go take a hot shower. Everything you need is in the closet, baby."

Eve smiled. "Bitch, you just don't know how much I love you," she said.

Coca licked her lips.

"Bitch, you got a nice round ass on you," Coca said.

Eve giggled. "Thank you, Coca baby."

"Hurry up with that shower, so we can hit *Club Thunder* and have a few drinks," Coca said.

Then she smirked. "You know what? I'ma take a shower with you."

"Okay, honey," Eve said, biting her lip.

Chapter 13

One night at *Club Thunder*, two cartels—Norteñas Blacks and Eastside Brotherhood—got into a bloody battle. Several major shots were fired in the middle of the club, hitting several gang members on both sides of the battle. People rushed underneath tables and into bathrooms for cover. In the midst of all this, Red got shot in her right shoulder while standing at the bar with a drink in her hand, talking to her friend Mimi.

Blood dripped down Red's shoulder as she screamed out in pain, begging for help. Mimi, seeing all that blood, passed out on the spot.

Karla rushed over to the bar and grabbed Red off the floor. "Bitch, let's get the hell out of here before the police arrive. You know a bitch still on federal papers. To be honest I'm not trying to get caught up in here and get violated to head back to Federal prison. You feel me?" Karla asked.

"Bitch, I hear you, damn. Don't hurt my arm bitch. You got to handle me gently. Where's your .40 Glock at so I can shoot this whole place up since somebody shot me in the shoulder," Red said, grinning through the pain.

"Hoe, please. You crazy as hell." Karla shook her head.

Mimi slowly sat up from the floor, dazed. "Damn, what happened?" she asked.

"Bitch, you passed the fuck out on the floor at the sight of Red's blood. It appears you're hemophobic," Karla said.

"Okay," Mimi mumbled.

They rushed out the nightclub, trying to avoid more trouble.

As they made it to the car, the club owner got on the speakers:

"EVERYBODY GET DOWN ON THE FLOOR!"

Red, Mimi and Karla jumped into their car, slammed it into reverse, and peeled out, bumping into parked cars as they sped off toward the hospital. Red was in so much pain it was pitiful.

Police swarmed Club Thunder, sirens blaring. There were so many law enforcement vehicles headed toward the club.

Detective Nene was called to the crime scene to see if any drugs or murders were involved.

Nene was the inside plug for most drug dealers, always letting them know what the Drug Task Force was planning before they even made a move. If the feds were talking about a raid, Nene would notify the cartels and local dealers. She was on payroll with plenty of them.

When Nene arrived at the scene, she got straight to work, no games.

She started asking different people questions, trying to see what information was useful and what could be tossed aside.

Nene walked toward the bar.

When she looked down, she spotted a handgun with blood on it.

She reached into her kit, grabbed a pair of red gloves, and picked the gun up.

"Hold up," one of the officers called out.

Another officer placed shell markers to log where the bullets and other evidence were found.

As Nene was working, a woman walked up to an officer nearby.

"Hey, sir."

The officer looked up. "Hey, Miss Lady. How are you?"

"I'm great right now, but I see you could use some help," the woman said, turning her gaze from Nene's co-worker to Nene.

The woman leaned in.

"I got some information about the shooting inside the club. Is there any way I can contact you privately? I don't wanna get hurt over the shit I'm about to tell you."

Nene nodded. "Yes."

She took off her gloves, reached into her pocket, and pulled out a business card.

"You can call me anytime. What's your name?" Nene asked.

The woman hesitated.

"I'll tell you later."

Then she turned and walked away, her red dress hugging her curves, high heels dangling from her hands.

Nene watched her go.

Then, she looked at her co-worker. "Damn, Sam . . . this woman might be helpful to this case—probably many more."

"Yep," Sam replied.

After processing the crime scene by the bar, Nene and Sam headed toward the back of the club.

Nene opened the backroom door—

And froze.

"Oh shit!" Nene screamed.

A Black woman lay on the floor—naked.

A knife was lodged in her chest . . . and another in her forehead.

Nene had been working with the Blytheville Police Department for twenty years, and she had never seen something like this.

Blood covered the walls.

The woman's body looked brutalized.

"Damn, Sam . . . this shit is serious," Nene muttered.

"Hell yeah."

Sam shook his head.

"Whoever did this wanted her dead real bad . . . to do her like this."

Nene sighed, reaching for her phone.

"Let me call the coroner."

She pulled her phone from her pocket and dialed.

"Hello?" Nene said.

A voice answered. "This is the Blytheville Coroner."

"This is Detective Nene Williams with the Blytheville PD Crime Unit. We got a young Black woman stabbed in the chest and forehead inside Club Thunder. I need you to come out to the scene."

"Understood. I'll be there as soon as possible. Will someone be there to let me in?"

"Yeah, the club owner and several officers will be here."

"Okay. Thank you, Detective Williams."

The call ended.

Nene put her phone back in her pocket, then turned to look at the body again.

Something wasn't right about this.

This wasn't just some random club fight.

It was deeper.

And Nene needed to find out why.

"Let's get the hell out of here before we run into more dead bodies in this club. Ah, let me tell the owner that the coroner is on his way and that officers will still be on the scene. Sam, you know a bitch is tired as hell right now." Nene sighed.

"Shit, me too, Nene. I need to get home to my family." Sam replied.

"These cartel wars getting worse out here in these streets. I'm still working on the Rambo and Buffy case because nobody's in jail for their deaths yet." Nene said.

She knew everything that was going on, but she was playing dumb with Sam.

She smirked to herself.

***

"Bambi, I need you to grab a 9mm, two AK-47s, and SKs and put them in the car. Pack up the rest of the guns, but leave one AR-15 out. And make sure you grab this duffle bag too," Marco ordered as he headed into the bathroom to take a shit.

Bambi went outside and loaded everything into the car like she was told. She opened the duffle bag and saw extra clips, money, and handguns inside.

"Damn, this nigga stay ready for war," he mumbled to herself, then zipped the bag back up, closed the car door, and headed back inside.

"Marco, you still in the bathroom?" Bambi called out.

"Yeah, baby. Something I ate didn't sit right with my stomach. I'll be done in a minute. You can go ahead and get in the car. I'll be out there soon."

Marco pulled out his cell phone and dialed Tonya—his side bitch.

After two rings, Tonya answered in a soft, sultry voice. "Hello."

"Baby, me and Bambi about to hit the highway. I need you to keep an eye on the crib while we gone. I'll Cash App you $1,500 in a minute just for your time. Don't let nobody know we leaving town, Tonya."

"Okay, I got you. But make sure you send that money. Is that big-ass dog put up somewhere?" Tonya asked.

"Yeah. My brother Kevin got him, so you straight."

"A'ight . . . Be safe. And don't give that bitch Bambi all my dick. When you gon' let me fuck Bambi with you?"

"Bitch, you crazy," Marco chuckled.

Click.

Marco cleared his phone history, just in case Bambi decided to go through his phone.

He walked out the bathroom, grabbed a bag of chips and a soda from the kitchen, then headed outside to the car. Sliding into the passenger seat, he kissed Bambi.

"What's up, honey?"

Bambi smirked, rubbing his bald head with her soft hands. "What you think, nigga? Coca's crew been hanging around Franklin Street, watching cars. Let's ride through the hood—see who out there."

Marco nodded, driving through the block at a slow pace.

When they pulled up on Franklin Street, they were shocked to see Coca and Eve posted up, talking to somebody.

Marco reached under the driver's seat, grabbed his Glock, and checked the clip.

He raised his gun—

And—just before he could pull the trigger—all you heard was:

BOOM! BOOM! BOOM!

"Ahh, shit!" Marco screamed.

The car swerved, then crashed into a light pole.

Coca kept firing her AR-15, lighting the car up.

Bambi ducked under the dashboard, but bullets tore through the car, hitting her in the chest and forehead.

"Help! Help!" Marco yelled.

Bambi choked on her own blood.

"I love you . . ."

Those were her last words.

Blood gushed from her body like a busted water pipe.

"Baby, don't die on me like this!" Marco sobbed.

His hands shook as he grabbed his .40 Glock, pressed it to his own head, and pulled the trigger.

Blood splattered everywhere.

Coca and her crew fled the scene.

They drove to the nearest river, tossing the guns out the window.

Then they sped off to their safe house, where they washed their hands with bleach and changed clothes.

This was something Coca and Eve would never forget.

They were born to kill.

"Bitch, you that killer!" Eve laughed.

After changing, they drove out to the country, taking their bloody clothes to an open field far out.

They set the trash bag on fire.

Eve grinned, watching the flames rise.

"Bitch, we got them hoes! This world belongs to us now!" She fired her AR-15 into the air, still hyped off the kill.

"Now that this shit is over, I can go back to college and live a normal life." Coca sighed.

Eve's eyes darkened. She turned to Coca, pointing the AR-15 at her head. "Bitch, what about me? You know I'm your bottom bitch 'til the wheels fall off. If you leave me . . . you a dead bitch."

Coca stiffened. "What you . . . you . . ."

She couldn't get her words out. She had always known Eve was crazy. From the moment she met her, she knew this bitch was unstable.

Coca forced a laugh. "Bitch, I'ma love your crazy ass 'til the day I die. You know that strap-on got your name written all over it—Big Pussy Eve."

Eve burst out laughing.

Coca sighed in relief.

The Blytheville Police Department arrived on Franklin Street after a local shooting was reported. A car had crashed into a pole, bullet holes riddling the entire vehicle. When officers peeked inside, they saw two dead bodies.

They grabbed their phones, calling for help.

"Oh my God," one of the officers said. "This is a sad sight at this moment," the officer said in a soft tone of voice.

Detective Nene arrived on the scene and recognized the bodies. She shook her head.

"This must've been a drug war gone bad," she said.

"Looks like it," an officer agreed.

Nene opened the driver's door, spotting weapons in the front and backseat. She reached into the backseat, grabbed a black duffle bag, and unzipped it.

Her eyes widened.

Money. Dope.

She quickly zipped the bag back up, masking her reaction. A white officer glanced over.

"What you got there, Nene?"

Nene turned, putting on her best straight face.

"Just more evidence. I'll take it in myself."

The officer nodded, not thinking twice. "Good. We need to wrap this up soon."

Nene walked to her car, tossing the bag in the passenger seat. As soon as she slid into the driver's seat, a slow grin crept across her face.

"Damn . . . this money gonna have me straight for a while," she said to herself, already knowing this bag was never making it to the evidence room.

A tall Black officer looked at Nene. "Hopefully help will be on the scene soon," he said, eyeing her up and down before walking down the street, looking for people to speak to about the crime.

"Okay. Here comes the ambulance," the short white officer said. The ambulance pulled up fast, medics rushing toward the bodies of Bambi and Marco. Merely looking at the bodies, they could tell that shit seemed bad at the time. They loaded them up, racing to the hospital—trying to save what was already dead.

Nene watched them drive off, then sighed. "Damn! They moved fast as hell. I need to go back to the station and handle some paperwork on a crime scene, including this one. That woman the other night at Club Thunder was supposed to call me with information. I will see you when you make it to the police station, John."

Nene opened her car door and slid into the driver's seat, cranking the engine. Just as she reached the gear shift, John leaned into the open window, resting his arms on the door.

His face was close now, just inches from hers. "A'ight, Nene. Take care."

He paused, his eyes locked on her. "But I really want some of that Black pussy, though."

Nene cut her eues at him, smirking.

John grinned, glancing down at her thick thighs. "I never had a Black woman with a fat-ass booty like you, Nene. I would love to eat that pussy first." His voice dropped lower, huskier. He smiled to himself, licking his lips.

Nene laughed, shaking to head. "This pussy cost, white boy." She threw her car in drive and sped off, leaving John standing there, watching her taillights fade down the street . She decided to go straight home instead of the police station. Nene was excited about the duffle bag she had in the car. She reached in her purse and grabbed her phone to call Coca. After about six rings, Coca finally picked up the phone. "Hello. Hello!" Nene kept saying.

"Hey, this Coca. I can hear you, damn."

"Girl, this Nene. I'm calling you to let you know that Bambi and Marco got murdered on the scene on Franklin Street. Many people claim they saw who did it, but you know a bitch like me was not paying any attention because you have me in your back pocket. Tomorrow, I need you to come by my crib so we can have a little one-on-one convo about my new contract. Make sure you dress to kill, bitch. We might go out to dinner." Nene said.

"Bitch, I'ma come over there butt-ass naked." Coca chuckled. Nawl "I'ma just joking. That's cool. I be over there tomorrow."

Damn, Nene must have some good news for me, Coca thought.

But she couldn't shake the *what-ifs*.

If anyone saw us kill Bambi and Marco, we might be in big trouble, maybe in some deep shit. Maybe even prison for a long-ass time. Coca sat there thinking hard.

Chapter 14

Red got released from the hospital after getting shot in the shoulder. She couldn't believe all the crazy shit that went down at Club Thunder that night, but she was thankful to still be alive.

When Red made it home, she went straight to her bedroom to grab some clothes for a shower.

Meanwhile, Karla was in the front room, playing a game on her phone, waiting on Red to finish up.

Karla's brother, Choppa, had already told her not to be going to *Club Thunder* because too much shit been going down there these past few weeks.

Karla put her phone down, then walked into the bathroom where Red was in the shower.

"Hey baby, it's Karla," she called out.

"Ahh, bitch! I thought you was somebody tryna kill me or rape me, the way you came in all quiet like that," Red said, catching her breath.

"Nawl, bitch." Karla grinned, then started stripping off all her clothes.

"Is it cool if I hop in with you? I need to clean this dirty-ass body," Karla asked.

"Yeah, it's cool, baby," Red replied.

"Ah, I forgot to grab some clothes for after I shower."

Karla rushed into the bedroom, digging through the dresser for something to put on. While she was searching, she reached under the bed and grabbed a small box. After grabbing it, she walked back into the bathroom, pulled back the shower curtain, and jumped in without saying a word.

The first thing Karla did was grab the bar of soap and a towel.

She started washing Red's body, being careful not to hurt her shoulder.

Then, Karla slid the soap down between Red's legs, pressing part of the bar inside her pussy.

"Ahh, shit, bitch!" Red moaned. "Bitch, that shit feel good as fuck."

Karla smirked. "Bitch, this feels good to you?"

Before Red could answer, Karla kissed her on the lips. Then, she slid her long middle finger inside Red's pussy, stroking back and forth without hesitation. Karla pulled her finger out, stuck it in her own mouth, then pushed it into Red's mouth.

"Bitch, let's take this to the bedroom and have a little fun," Red said, eyes full of excitement.

She jumped out the shower, barely drying off before running into the bedroom.

Karla followed right behind her, making sure she grabbed her strap-on in the process. Her pussy was already throbbing, craving Red's tongue on her clit, ready to let her juices flow down Red's throat.

Karla was a thick, nasty bitch who took dick in all parts of her body—including her anal hole.

"Baby, I'ma finna punish you," Karla growled as she walked into the bedroom with a mean-ass look on her face.

Red was in the bedroom, laid back on the bed with her legs wide open. She stuck her finger inside her pussy, making loud, wet noises that drove Karla crazy with excitement. "Baby, this pussy is ready for you," Red said.

"Oh yeah?" Karla reached down, unrolled the bath towel off her own body, revealing the strap-on in her hand.

"Oh my God, bitch!" Red screamed.

Karla took her time, putting on the strap-on nice and slow. But once she got it on, she started gripping it in her hand, moving it up and down, pointing it toward Red.

"You know sometimes I break hearts, right? Friends . . . lovers . . . don't matter. I fuck the dog shit outta them," Karla said, teasing her.

Red smirked, then licked her lips

"Karla, check the bottom drawer and grab that can of grease. I don't want you hurting this pussy—I ain't no young thot no more," Red said.

"Oh yeah. You not a turf bitch like that. You barely can take eight inches of plastic dick. Bitch, you crazy," Karla said, smirking. She grabbed the grease from the bottom drawer and rubbed most of it on the plastic dildo to make sure it would be slick going inside Red. Karla scooped more grease from the can and rubbed it over Red's pussy, making sure she was ready. Red was already wet as a river down there when Karla rubbed Red's pussy with her hand. The moment Karla touched her clit, Red's body jerked slightly.

"Here we go," Karla said. She lined up the head of the strap-on and slowly pushed it inside Red's wet pussy.

"Hell yeah. Bitch, hold up one minute. You trying to murder me, bitch, in here," Red gasped.

"Red I don't have the whole thing inside yet. Take this dick, bitch, and chill. Your pussy already wet," Karla said, gripping Red's hips as she eased deeper, pushing more plastic inside Red's pussy.

Before Red could protest again, Karla was fast-stroking Red back and forth, gripping her thighs. She snatched Red's left leg up, pinned it in the air, pounding and pounding her to the fullest.

"Bitch, how you like this?" Karla asked, slapping Red's ass.

"Bitch, I'ma pro in this shit. Give me this dick." Red grabbed the dildo and pushed it deeper inside her pussy.

"Damn, this feels good to me, but it hurts a little," she admitted.

"Hold up," Karla said.

Karla pulled out, dropped to her knees, and buried her face between Red's legs. She stuck her tongue deep inside Red's pussy, licking her from the inside out.

Red's legs trembled as she tried to hold still, but Karla gripped her hips tight.

Karla's tongue ring flicked against Red's clit umpteen times, making her moan louder.

Then Karla slid lower, letting her tongue trace circles around Red's asshole. She flicked her tongue, then pushed it deep inside.

"You like that?" Karla asked.

"Ahhh . . . mmm . . . baby, you the best," Red moaned, gripping the sheets.

Karla raised back up, sticking her tongue deeper inside Red's wetness, and started. tongue-fucking Red's pussy like she'd stolen something and was being punished at the moment.

Twisting and turning, Red's body was moving uncontrollably. "Bitch, you about to make me cum. I want you to lick all this nut off my pussy. Oh, shit, bitch!" Red screamed.

"Bitch, don't cum yet," Karla ordered. She raised up, licking red's juices off her own lips, savoring the taste. Then she climbed to the front of the bed, spreading Red's legs wider to have full access to her pretty pussy even more. Red kept that pussy bald down there, and it smelled like strawberries.

Karla sucked on the lips of Red's pussy, then spread Red ass cheeks apart so she could eat that pussy how she really wanted to.

Red didn't even move. She was either tired or faking, just to keep Karla doing what she was doing.

Karla licked in Red's crease, then sucked on Red's clit while sliding three fingers inside her wetness. The sound of it—the slurping, the splashing—filled the room.

Red started squirming, moaning louder and louder.

"Mmmm, oh shit baby. You making me wetter now," Red said.

Karla grinned. She spread Red's pussy lips apart and licked it like a cat licking milk out of a bowl.

Red trembled.

"Don't trying make me go crazy around here about you, bitch. You know you a bitch feeling like a star right now," Red said.

Karla kept fingering Red's pussy, sucking on her clit, while whispering dirty shit to her. She kissed Red's ass cheeks, spreading them apart, then slid her tongue back into her asshole. Red backed her thick ass up on Karla's tongue. Karla spread Red's ass wider this time, licking the crease.

Red let out a scream like she had just hit the winning shot at a basketball game.

"Hell yeah. You are driving a bitch insane," Red gasped. She arched her back, gyrating her thick ass into Karla's face.

Karla grabbed Red by the hips, pulling her up on all fours like a trick bitch at a strip club on Brooks Road. Then she pressed her face deep into Red's ass crease, her tongue sliding inside that tight hole.

"Karla I wanna taste you," Red said, panting.

"Not right now," Karla said. She stopped eating Red's pussy, moved around to the other side of the bed, and guided the long strap-on into Red's warm mouth.

Red sucked it with no hands, like a pro in this shit. Karla gripped her head and moved the strap-on in and out of her mouth.

"Baby, let me fuck you some more, Dirty Red," Karla whispered.

Red laid back, spread her legs wide, and let Karla slide the strap-on deep inside her pussy.

Karla pushed in deeper, filling Red's tightness. She just held it there for a second, kissed Red's lips, and sucked on them like an apple lollipop.

Red wrapped her legs around Karla's waist, pulling her closer.

Karla kissed on Red's neck while Red gyrated on the strap-on.

Karla moved in and out, stroking deep, while Red moaned and licked her lips.

"Damn, this feel like I won the lottery tonight with you. The drinks and the weed got a bitch feeling good. And the pain don't even hurt as much," Red said.

Karla smirked. She pushed Red's knees up to her chest. This act made Red put her feet against Karla's chest. Then, Karla dropped dick in her, over and over.

"Cum with me, bitch!" Red screamed.

Karla could feel Red's pussy gripping onto the strap-on, clenching tight, like it was stuck for dear life.

"I'ma about to bust, bitch," Red panted.

"Bitch, make it happen." Karla stroked harder, deeper, hitting her guts.

"Yes, yes! Bitch, you belong to me," Karla growled. She kept beating Red's pussy until Red screamed out louder and louder.

And then came that special word.

"Baby, you my love forever. I'll die for you . . . Ahh shit, this feel good . . . I'ma cumming! Ohhh shit—hell yeah! Damn, bitch!" Red moaned, body shaking.

Karla rolled Red onto the bed, both of them breathing heavy.

They laid there for a while, silent.

"Baby, I love you. You my everything," Red whispered.

Karla turned her head, smirking. "I love you too. Good night."

Chapter 15

Nene decided to go to the police station to do a little studying on the case at *Club Thunder* and Franklin Street. As she walked into the station, John greeted her with a smile.

"How you doing, sir?" Nene asked.

"Well, I'ma doing okay, now that I see my co-worker." John was so excited he couldn't keep his eyes off Nene's titties and thick thighs.

Both of them walked upstairs to their workstations.

On Mondays, nobody came to work but Nene and John.

John had a mad crush on Nene.

Nene stood up and walked into the other office.

John was looking so hard, his dick got hard in his pants. He decided to follow behind her, moving like a dog chasing a cat. Once John made it into the office where Nene was, he spoke up.

"Hey Nene, how much it gonna cost to have a nice time with you for about an hour or two?" John asked.

"What the fuck you saying? An hour or two? Nigga, you trippin' like hell! This pussy cost you your life, fuckin' with a bitch like me. Your dick might be too little to even get up in this pussy." Nene smirked, making her point clear.

She reached out, grabbing John's dick, making him smile even harder. Then, she started playing with his dick through his pants with her small hands.

"John, your dick too little the way it feel down here."

John chuckled.

"You know, the last Black girl that said that—I punished her pussy for two hours straight."

Nene laughed. "Boy, please! You talkin' about fuckin' me for two hours straight? Boy, please."

John grinned, already taking off his clothes, piece by piece.

"You ready for this?" he asked.

"Hold up, white boy. Where the money at?" Nene asked.

John reached into his back pocket, pulled out his wallet, and took out five one-hundred-dollar bills, handing them to Nene.

"This enough for a couple hours? I just wanna have a good time," John said.

Nene snatched the money.

"I guess so, player of the year."

She grabbed John's dick, examined it for a second, then stopped and started removing her clothes right there in the office.

Nene's pussy was shaved bald, her big pearl tongue clit poking out.

"You see all this pussy, John?" She grabbed her pussy again, smiling at him.

"Damn, you thick as hell! Thicker than a two-dollar Snickers bar at a candy store.

I'ma have a lot of fun with you in this office. Maybe I can make you touch everything in here, fuckin' you in all sorts of positions. I'ma show you how a white boy get down, Nene."

John grinned, stepping closer.

Nene grabbed his dick, placed it inside her mouth, and started deep-throating it back and forth like she had a license to eat dick. Her mouth got wetter and wetter, her tongue circling the tip of his dickhead.

Then she did her signature move.

She reached into her purse, pulled out a condom, tore it open with her teeth, and slid it into her mouth. Without using her hands, she rolled the condom onto his dick with just her lips and tongue.

She started sucking his dick for a good ten minutes before she hopped on the officer's desk, pushing everything out the way. Laying on her back, she spread her thick legs apart and started fingering her pussy, the wet sound echoing through the air.

"Damn, baby, hold up with that." John grabbed his dick and placed it inside Nene's pussy.

Her pussy was so deep and long inside, she didn't even make a sound—Not until John started jumping up and down in her guts like he was playing basketball.

"Ahh shit! Fuck! You got a bitch going crazy over this dick! Ahh shit! You in a bitch stomach right now!" Nene moaned.

John flipped Nene over into a crazy position, then stuck his long tongue deep inside her asshole. He moved fast, back and forth, making Nene moan so loud he had to put his hand over her mouth to quiet her down. "This tongue the best in town, Nene," John bragged. Then, he grabbed his dick and inserted it into her pussy.

Nene jumped, screaming for help.

"Damn, I never fucked a white man before neither," she moaned. "You havin' your way with me right now. Come on, white man, make this pussy cum to the fullest!"

Nene started throwing her pussy back at him, making John hit her harder, stroke after stroke.

"Baby, you can have anything I own. I'ma make sure your rent, car note, and bills stay paid."

John kept punishing Nene's pussy.

"Oh shit! Damn, right there! Ohhh shit! I'ma cumming! Oh fuck! Damn, you got a bitch wet as fuck right now!"

John lowered his big mouth to her pussy and sucked all the extra cum up.

Nene squirmed on the desk like a fish outta water.

Then, all of a sudden—

Nene started squirting all over the place.

"Baby, let's get dressed before somebody walk in on us," John said and wiped his mouth, grinning. "Now, I can finally say I busted a nut on a Black woman's pussy. You see all this dick right here?"

"Yes, daddy," Nene purred.

"It belongs to you and no other woman."

John grabbed his dick, jacking it off in front of Nene's face.

Nene lowered her head, ready to catch his nut.

"Ahh shit, here it comes, baby!" John groaned.

"Hold up," Nene said. She made sure she was in position to catch every drop before it hit the floor.

"Ah shit, bitch! Here it go—"

SPLASH!

John's cum shot inside Nene's mouth, the rest painting her face like a signature.

Nene coughed as the cum rushed down her throat. She wiped it off with her hands, then laughed like she was crazy. She stuck her tongue out, sucking up the extra nut.

John chuckled, grabbing his shirt and handing it to her.

"You a nasty bitch!"

"Thank you. Yes, I'ma nasty and dirty," Nene said, wiping her pussy and face with his shirt.

John snatched the shirt back and put it on. "Baby, I gotta get outta here," he said, pulling his clothes on fast.

Nene started getting dressed too. "Damn, you got a bitch sore as hell. I need to go home and take a nice, hot shower," she sighed.

She kissed John on the lips, and he palmed her round ass with both hands.

Once they were fully dressed, they headed out the office, walked through the police station, and went their separate ways.

"Bye, Big Dick Daddy!" Nene called out.

"Bye, Nene."

John grinned, getting into his car.

***

The next morning, Nene called John to come by her crib to look at some files that might help solve several murder cases around town.

Ten minutes later, John arrived.

Knock! Knock! Knock!

Nene ran to the front door and opened it without saying a word.

Then, she reached straight down to John's dick in his pants.

Just by the way her hands felt, she had him hard as a brick of cocaine turning into crack rock.

Nene unzipped his pants and pulled his dick out. She moved her nightcoat out the way, turned her thick ass up on him backwards, and slid his rock-hard dick right inside her.

"Oh shit, Nene. This pussy feel so good right now," John moaned.

Nene moved back and forth, making waves all around them. She gripped his arms, using them to pull herself back onto his dick.

"Damn, this dick bigger than a bitch thought! I couldn't get enough of this dick yesterday at work," she moaned.

John ignored her words, stroking her harder and deeper.

His focus was handling business.

"Oh shit, John!"

Nene bounced her round ass onto his dick even faster. "Baby, I love this white dick.

Please don't ever keep it from me," she begged.

"You a beautiful Black woman with class. You deserve to be loved and respected at all times," John whispered. He sped up the pace, squeezed onto her ass cheeks, and stroked in and out of her pussy harder and harder.

Their bare skin slapped together, sounding like a crowd clapping at a basketball game after someone made a basket.

"I'm cumming, baby! I'm cumming on this large dick! Damn, white boy John, this dick so, so good to a bitch! Oh shit, Big Daddy!" Nene screamed.

She smashed her ass into John, and they both came at the same time.

John pulled his dick out and put it away.

Nene turned around, grinning.

"I never punished a Black woman like this before, Nene."

"Yeah . . . That was some wild bullshit we just did—With my oldest son in the bedroom!

I wanted this dick so bad, I took a chance to get fucked. Can you put all that dick in my stomach?"

"Will do, baby," John replied.

"John, I'ma give you a sample of what you been missing . . . Since the last time we was together at the job."

"Is that right, Nene? I can't wait for you to suck on this dick . . . While I eat your pussy."

"John, that's called 69. Most people do it when they wanna be fair to both partners. You about to make me say fuck that detective job," Nene joked.

"Nene, you wild as hell," John laughed.

"John, I called you over to thank you for eating this pussy good yesterday. Fuck the files.

I wanted some dick."

Nene dropped to her short knees, pulled John's dick out, and wrapped her hands around it. She pumped his dick three times, then kissed the tip of his dickhead. Then, she licked it until it was fully erect. She kept sucking and licking, grabbing his big nuts at the same time.

"Get nasty with this dick like you hit the lottery. Ummm, baby, suck this dick. I won't tell nobody you a freaky bitch," John groaned.

"Yes . . . Yes . . ." Nene moaned.

She pulled his dick between her breasts and squeezed them tight.

Then, she used her titties to stroke his dick, while she licked the tip of his dickhead with her long tongue.

"Nene! Damn! Shit! This shit feel so good. I'm about to cum, baby. Ohhh shit, I'm cumming, Black Queen!"

John nutted all over her face and in her hair.

"John, I never had this much fun with a white man. You know we can't let nobody at work know we fuckin'. We both can lose our jobs in a heartbeat. Maybe we can hook up later, on a day off."

Knock! Knock! Knock!

There was someone at the front door.

They grabbed their clothes, throwing them on fast. John jumped into the bedroom closet. Nene walked out the bedroom, into the front room, then toward the front door.

"Who is it?" she asked.

"It's me, Karla, at the door, bitch!" Karla screamed.

Nene opened the door.

"How you doing, Karla?"

"I'm okay," Karla said.

"I was about to take a shower before you knocked, coming over without calling first. At least you shoulda called a bitch first."

"Girl, please. I'm on my thug shit."

Karla flopped down on the couch.

Nene sat across from her, legs wide open, wearing only a white T-shirt, her bald pussy on full display.

"There's so much shit going on out here, Karla. As you may not know, you will never go to prison if I have anything to do with it. Right now, the murders on Franklin and at *Club Thunder* been my main concern to sweep under the rug. The officers tried to ask me questions about you and Red, but I told them when those murders happened, you was in Memphis shopping at the mall. Right now, I gotta text Cuz and let him know they thinking about raiding him Monday at his home on the west side," Nene said.

She grabbed her cell phone off the table and texted her Cuz, Mike, to inform him about what's about to go down Monday.

"Okay, now let's get to business since I'm done texting Cuz, friend," Nene said.

"Hey! Do you have any dope, guns, or money you took from any drug dealers on the street?" Karla asked.

John eased his way out the bedroom closet, listening to the conversation.

Then, he slipped out the back door into his car.

"Well, you know a bitch got you. When I first started selling drugs in the projects, my uncle gave me several twenty rocks, and for each one I sold, I made a five-dollar profit. At times, my friends and I would sell crack to junkies on the block or even when they pulled up in the alley. We would run to them to sell what we had, and most of the time, we ended up getting into fights behind that. It got so bad that white junkies would ask to see how big the crack rocks were in our hands, and all of a sudden, they'd slap our hands, knocking the rocks into their car, then speed off. Coming up in the hood wasn't easy at all, as you can hear from my story. Over time, saving up little money to buy clothes, shoes, food, and go to football games wasn't enough to keep buying the shit I wanted. A man saw how hard I hustled and decided to give me a chance to grow bigger in the dope game. Many times, my mother would send me next door to ask the neighbors for sugar, bread, or a couple of dollars until the first of the month when my parents got their welfare check. She had credit with the local white folks' store in the hood, but she still tried to save money. I ended up getting a part-time job at Sonic to help out around the house. As years passed, things changed."

Nene broke down crying.

"Nene, things gonna be okay. Look at you now—you successful. Most people don't make it out the hood like you,

Nene. You kept going, stayed in college, and soon, you'll have a degree in Criminal Justice."

Karla kissed Nene on the forehead and held her soft hands to make her feel better.

"Hey, Mama! I'ma run down the road, I'll be back later," Nene's son yelled from the backroom. He walked out the back door and saw a car pulling off from the front of the house.

Karla and Nene walked into the bedroom and sat down.

Karla smiled, seeing that Nene was feeling better.

But Nene's shirt was wet from her tears. She kept wiping them away while Karla kept looking down between her legs.

Karla massaged Nene's shoulders, placed a kiss on her neck, then eased her hands between Nene's legs. She rubbed Nene's pussy, back and forth, making Nene moan.

"You like that, Nene?" Karla asked.

"Hell yeah, bitch! You wanna eat this pussy or what, Karla?"

Nene laid on her back, opening her legs wide for enjoyment. She stuck her middle finger inside her own pussy, moving it back and forth. Then, she pulled her fingers out and stuck them inside her own mouth.

"Karla, I could use a good cat lick right now," Nene teased.

"Bitch, you crazy," Karla smirked. "Bitch, this tongue gon' make you shoot cum like an AR-15 in a war in the middle of the hood. You blessed to be in shape like you are. That pussy nice and shaved."

Karla kept talking crazy shit, but she was mad as hell that her sex toys were still inside her car.

"Nene, I need to go get something out my car. You gon' be ready by the time I come back in?"

"Okay. I'ma be right here waiting," Nene said, rising up from the bed.

Karla rushed out the bedroom to her car.

Nene looked through her bedroom closet for something special to put on, but she couldn't find shit. She just took off her t-shirt and jumped back into bed, under the covers, waiting on Karla to return.

"This bitch don't know—if she brings a strap-on, she better let me use it on her too."

Nene jumped out the bed, walked to the bathroom, and checked to see if John was still in the house.

He wasn't there.

She rushed back into the bedroom, looking under the bed to see if he was hiding under there.

Nothing.

Then, she checked out the side window to see if John's car was still outside.

But it was gone.

"Damn. John left. I wanted to have a threesome with him," Nene said.

Karla made it to her car. She reached under the driver's seat for her toolbox.

Shit—her phone started ringing.

She looked at it—Red.

Karla answered. "Hello?"

"Hey, baby, what you doin'?" Red asked.

"I'm at Nene house, talkin' to her about somethin' dealin' with the files she got. You know a bitch can't talk too much over the phone."

"Whatever, bitch. You probably tryna fuck that snake-ass bitch. I bet not catch you. If I do—you and that bitch dead."

"Baby, stop trippin' on me all the time. You should trust me by now."

Karla kept gathering her tools, then slammed the driver's door closed.

"Let me finish talkin' to Nene. You welcome to come by."

Karla was playin' mind games with Red to see what she would say.

"I'm cool," Red said, but at the same time, she was gettin' dressed to hit a few blocks around the hood.

"Well, I'll talk to you later, baby."

"Okay.

Love you, Dirty Red."

Karla laughed after making that crazy comment.

"Bye, bitch. Love you too, Karla C—"

Red hung up.

Karla walked back inside the house, toolbox in hand, never thinking about locking the front door.

She rushed into the bedroom and sat the small toolbox next to the bed on the floor.

Karla took off all her clothes and jumped into bed with Nene.

She kissed Nene on the lips and slid a finger inside her pussy.

"Oh shit, bitch! You workin' that one finger inside a bitch right now. We supposed to be talkin' about gettin' money, not fuckin' on each other at this moment. You know I got several duffle bags full of drugs that I need you to push back on the streets soon. Karla, you can sell them bricks of cocaine at a low price to build up your customers out here."

"Yes, yes, baby," Karla whispered.

She kept pushin' her finger deeper inside Nene.

"Yes, yes, baby!" Nene screamed.

"Nene, I need all the drugs you got right now." Karla pulled her fingers out and grabbed her small toolbox, getting her strap-on ready.

Nene looked shook in the face.

"Can you take all this dick, Nene?" Karla asked. "I ain't gon' break nothin' inside your pussy. You probably need a good fuckin' anyway."

Karla grabbed the plastic strap-on, waved it at Nene.

"Yes! I can take that and more, bitch!"

Nene spread her pussy wide open with her hands.

Karla jumped onto the bed and laid on her back.

The strap-on pointed straight up at the ceiling.

She smiled at Nene in a sexy way, gripping the strap-on and waving it from side to side.

"Ahh yeah."

Nene jumped right on top of Karla and slid the strap-on inside her pussy without a problem.

She bounced up and down on the long plastic dick like a basketball hittin' the gym floor.

"This shit feels excellent!"

She sped up the pace, ridin' it in different positions.

Nene put her hands on Karla's small chest as her pussy started leakin' pre-cum on the strap-on.

"Damn, this is amazing! I ain't never felt this good before! This my big dick, and don't fuck nobody with it!"

Nene realized she was callin' the strap-on a dick because it looked long and hard like one.

"Baby, fuck me from the back," Nene said, jumping around, gettin' in position. She smacked her own ass cheeks. "C'mon and fuck this pussy tough, bitch!"

"Bitch, please!" Karla shoved the long strap-on inside Nene, making her moan through the air.

She stroked harder and harder, with so much force that caused pictures to fall off the walls.

She grabbed Nene's long weave, pulling chunks out.

They was fuckin' so hard, both of them lost control and didn't even realize what they was doin'.

Meanwhile, Red had pulled up in front of the house, sittin' in her car, listenin' to music.

Karla flipped Nene over, spreadin' her legs apart, and rammed the strap-on inside her again. She went so fast, shit kept fallin' over, and Nene screamed for dear life.

"Please stop! Please, baby, please! I won't do it no more, Karla!" Nene screamed.

But Karla kept poundin' her.

Nene grabbed the sheets—and a handful of Karla's weave.

"Bitch, don't snatch my weave out! This shit cost me $400 at the beauty store on Main Street!"

Nene smiled— but not for long.

"Oh shit! I'm cumming! Oh—ahh—here it gooooooes!"

Nene felt like a rocket launchin' off a ship. Her pussy was soaked.

"Lemme suck the rest of my cum off your dick?" Nene grabbed the strap-on and slid it into her mouth, deep-throatin' it fast. Then, she jumped off the bed into a chair, spreadin' her legs apart.

Karla rammed the strap-on inside her so fast, Nene's head bumped the wall several times.

Karla kept poundin' and poundin' while Nene screamed like somebody shot her with a handgun.

Red eased into the house through the front door, her handgun on her waist like always. She heard a woman screaming and moaning.

But something was off.

"That ain't Karla's voice. It sound like another bitch," Red spoke out loud.

She crept up closer to the bedroom door.

Inside the Bedroom—

"Yes, baby, right there! Put that dick in my stomach!"

Nene's voice filled the room.

Red grabbed the bedroom doorknob—then, all of a sudden . . .

"Oh, shit! Ahh, hell yeah! Fuck me, Karla!"

Karla was stroking Nene so hard, her pussy was makin' all kinds of nasty-ass sounds.

Neither one of them realized Red was in the room.

Karla pushed in deeper—like she just hit a home run in a baseball game.

Then, she glanced up.

And froze.

Red was standin' right there, inside the bedroom, starin' at them.

She had that killer mode face.

Karla was shocked—but kept strokin' Nene.

"Ain't this 'bout a bitch! You bitches coulda invited me to join. Go 'head—keep fuckin' her just like you been doin'. I wanna hear them sounds, see that facial expression on Nene's face. Maybe a bitch can join the sex team now."

Red started takin' off her clothes. She grabbed her handgun off her waist, wrapped it in her shirt, and placed it on the floor.

Now, she was fully undressed.

"Damn, Red, you look like a snack right now," Nene said, turnin' her head in Red's direction, while still gettin' dicked down.

"You want some of this pussy, Dirty Red?" Nene asked.

"Hell yeah! Lemme finish you up. You know I got my own strap-on in the car outside."

Red slipped on her dress, but no panties, and walked outside to her car.

She opened the back door, reached in, and grabbed her toolbox.

Red held the strap-on up, smirking.

Then, she closed the car door and headed back inside.

***

"Oh my God! I'm cumming! Here it gooooes! Bitch, you got a hoe sore right now!" Nene grabbed her pussy, cum drippin' everywhere.

"It's a must Red fuck me next— if that's cool with you, Karla?"

Nene climbed into bed, takin' a short break.

Red made it back inside, walkin' in like she owned the place. She had gone to the car dressed, but now—nothing but that fat pussy on display because she'd taken off her panties the instant she got back inside. Her pussy looked so swollen, like a bee had stung her between her legs. She had the fattest pussy Nene had ever seen.

"Damn, Karla, you done fucked the shit outta Nene already?"

Red pulled out her strap-on. "Now, bitch—it's my time to have some fun." She grabbed Nene's legs, spread 'em wide, and dove her head between them. Her tongue glided back and forth over Nene's wet pussy.

Karla sat in a chair watchin' the whole thing, seein' some new shit unfold before her eyes.

This was new.

She and Red had never fucked the same bitch at the same time.

But Red?

She was eatin' that pussy like a free buffet meal at a church service dinner.

"Eat this pussy, bitch!" Nene clapped her legs together, squeezin' Red's head tight to enjoy the pleasure. "Bitch, I'm 'bout to cum all in your mouth! To the fullest!"

Karla couldn't take it anymore.

She got up, got behind Red, and shoved the strap-on inside her.

Red paused for a minute—but then went right back to eatin'.

"Oh baby, you hurtin' me!" Red tried to scream, but Karla couldn't hear shit.

Red's head was buried too deep between Nene's thighs. She finally pulled away, gasping for air. Then, she grabbed the strap-on, guided it to Nene's pussy, and shoved it in.

Karla felt left out. "Damn, bitch! You just pushed me out the way completely?"

"Yeah, lemme handle this bitch! You been fuckin' Nene all day. I wanna see how much of these twelve inches she can take."

Red pushed in deeper.

"Well, I'ma take a walk to the bathroom," Karla said.
But really—
She was tryna check out the house.
See what kinda money she could make off this shit.
She stepped into the guest room, started searching . . .
Looked under the bed—
Found a yellow note.
She picked it up and read it:
"You will always be a part of me. Even though you never dated a white man in your lifetime, I want to tell you that I am married and have several kids. You can be my side thot. Love you always, Nene baby."
Karla froze.
The fuck!
Nene fuckin' her white co-worker?
A white man with kids?
She couldn't believe it.
She dropped the note on the floor—
Then, picked it back up and slid it back under the mattress before continuing to search.

***

Red stared down at the creamy package of goddess layin' on the sheets.
She had just dug the shit outta Nene, and tasting Nene on her tongue was the sweetest thing she had ever done.
Red wanted Nene bad.
The way Nene wrapped her legs around Red's head made Red crazy insane.
Red's mouth latched onto her nipples without a doubt.
She fucked Nene slow and deep, pulling out a couple of times—just so she could go deeper all over again.
Nene laid back on the bed, while Red stood over her, watching.
Then, Nene sucked the strap-on into her mouth.

125

She gripped the strap with the rim of her lips and tickled Red's asshole with her finger.

Slurping and purring, Nene opened her throat as Red fucked her mouth.

Nene wanted to suck all night, but Karla was still somewhere in the house.

Red extracted her joint from Nene's mouth and ran the tip of the head lightly over her lips. She slid the strap-on down Nene's neck, over to her left breast. Rubbing the wet head over her nipples.

Red fucked them beautiful, plump breasts with passion.

Nene gasped and moaned, her breasts getting even fuller, nipples hardening into miniature stones.

"Beat these titties up, baby!"

Nene lifted both breasts toward Red, gripping the strap-on and lightly slapping her nipples back and forth.

Red held the strap like a real dick, slapping, rubbing, and flicking Nene's nipples— until Nene came, arching her back and crying out Red's name.

Red was in total control.

She pushed Nene's legs open wide and entered her again.

Red fucked Nene with gentle passion and desperate need, making sure she covered all her spots and hit the back of her pussy with firm, deep strokes.

She made Nene cum long and hard, time and time again.

Red's heart beat fast against Nene's soft, sticky breasts. She had never felt better in her life.

Where the hell is Karla? Nene thought.

"Damn, where that bitch Karla at? She been gone a minute now," Red asked.

"Shit, I don't know! You been fuckin' the shit outta me in here, Red."

Nene laughed, breathin' hard. "Hopefully, Karla ain't hear me screamin' through the house like a bitch."

Red shook her head, smirkin'. "Nene, you a damn trip, girl."

She removed her strap-on and stood up, stretching. "Can I use your bathroom?"

"Yes, you sexy as hell, Red," Nene replied in a sultry tone.

Red grinned. "Thank you, baby."

She grabbed her strap-on, walked toward the bathroom, and looked around for something to clean it with.

She spotted a small basket full of towels, grabbed one along with a bar of soap sittin' on the side of the tub.

After about three minutes, she threw the dirty towel into the basket and walked back into the bedroom.

Karla was still nowhere to be found.

"Nene, I gotta run to my house real quick to check on something."

Red started puttin' her clothes on. "Bitch, we gotta do this again soon. Next time, I'll let you fuck me."

Nene raised an eyebrow. "Is that right?" She smirked. "Bitch, I'ma have you walkin' crazy around this house."

Nene grabbed Red's chin, pulled her close, and kissed her deep before watchin' her head out.

She heard the front door shut, then licked her lips.

Damn, Red cute and thick. It's a must I fuck her with this strap-on. She has a huge pussy—probably can take the whole ten inches, Nene thought to herself, smirking.

She got up, started walkin' through the house, lookin' around. She headed into the kitchen, opened the closet.

Something felt off.

"Could a bitch be trippin' right now?" Nene mumbled to herself.

Meanwhile, at Karla's Crib…

Karla pulled up into her garage. She got out, opened the back door, and grabbed the duffle bags off the seat. She struggled with 'em at first— then, they slipped and hit the ground.

Karla sighed and wheeled the bags inside. She opened the first duffle bag— stacks of money. She zipped it back up, pushed it to the side. She grabbed the second duffle bag, unzipped it—nothing but files. Karla closed it back, placed it by the garage door.

She started to walk away—but stopped.

"Damn, a bitch almost forgot about the side pockets."

She unclipped one, unzipped it.

Four big-ass bags of cocaine.

Jackpot.

Just then—

A loud knock at the front door.

Karla jumped up, hurried to the front.

The door opened.

Red stood there, holdin' her house key.

"Bitch, you scared the hell outta me." Karla exhaled, puttin' a hand on her chest.

Red grinned. "Bitch, you left a hoe fuckin' Nene without you joinin' the action." She smirked. "Nene told me to tell you to bring the duffle bags back. She sent me a text—she worried about them files. She said you can keep the cash and dope, though."

"The duffle bags are in the hallway. Bitch, you scared me at the front door, so I moved 'em around."

Karla shrugged. "Right now, I'm tired as fuck. We gon' push some drugs on the block soon. You gon' have plenty of cash, just be patient, bitch."

She yawned. "I'ma head to bed. You comin' with me, Red baby?"

Red nodded. "Yeah."

She followed behind Karla.

Both of them jumped in the bed together, takin' a cat nap.

Karla had a grimy heart. She fucked up heads around the hood. She was manipulative and slick.

And so fucking beautiful.

She had the kinda body that busted straight outta her clothes.

They fell asleep holdin' each other.

Chapter 16

Coca left the trap house and hit the cut, headin' to her hideoff spot. As she walked up the long driveway, she noticed her front door wide open—the door frame all broken.

She posted up in the cut and called Nene's phone.

Nene answered on the third ring.

"What's good, baby?" Nene asked.

"Can you bring me a duffle bag full of handguns? Somebody broke into my hideout spot." Coca asked.

"Okay. Give me twenty minutes, I'll be there." Nene said.

Coca hung up.

She put all the money she had inside the next-door neighbor's trash can, just in case the intruders were still in the house and shit got crazy.

Coca been out hustlin' all day around the hood.

***

Baller hit the cut faster than Coca thought— his fat ass could move when he needed to. Coca snatched the AR-15 outta Baller's hands and sprinted toward the trap house.

The sun was beamin' extra hard, and the neighborhood was too quiet.

Baller was right behind Coca with two handguns.

Coca motioned for Baller to go 'round the back while she took the damaged front door.

She pushed the door open, then stood to the side, listening for movement.

Nothing.

But when she looked inside—

Eve was lyin' in a pool of blood.

"Damn, these heartless thugs killed my girlfriend," Coca muttered.

She bent down, kissed Eve's forehead, and tears started rollin' down her face.

"This is some bullshit!" Coca walked away, opened the back door, and let Baller inside.

They cleared the whole house.

Nobody.

Coca looked around.

The entire house was turned upside down.

She was mad as hell.

She turned back toward Eve. Her brains splattered across the walls. Bullet wounds all over her body.

"Coca, who all knew about this spot here?" Baller asked.

"Nobody but Nene. I ain't never told nobody to come over but that snake bitch." Coca lied through her teeth. "The safe spots were cut open. Whoever did this took their precious time—lookin' for somethin' specific."

"The kitchen closet was open?" Baller asked.

"Nah, but you can tell they was tryin' to get up on the roof. You know that spot locked down to the beam in the ceiling, so they ain't movin' shit. Get Shell over here to clean this house up. And have him fix the front door frame."

"I'm on it now, Coca. But what you gonna do about this spot now?"

Coca sighed. "I'ma use it to fuck my bitches and throw house parties. I got a new spot on the north side I grabbed a month ago—just in case some shit like this went down."

She walked back up through the house, her mind racing.

Coca wasn't mad about the break-in.

But killing Eve?

That was a different ball game.

Eve was the most beautiful woman she ever had. She came into Coca's life with so much joy and happiness.

Somebody was gonna answer for this shit.

"Once again, think back to all the people you had over here. How many bitches you had over here?" Baller asked.

"Not many, player. I had Nene here the other day. We fucked, then she went to take a hot shower. All of a sudden, I started lookin' for my duffle bags—couldn't find 'em. Once Nene got out the shower, she was lookin' nervous as hell. She saw me searchin' the house and started askin' me all sorts of questions."

"This low-down bitch!" Baller said.

"What you gonna do about it?" Coca asked.

"You'll see. Just hold on, baby." Baller said.

Coca walked by the neighbor's house, reached in the trash can, and got her belongings. She walked to her car, put the bag in the trunk, then hopped in.

Baller jumped in the passenger seat, a crazy look on his face.

Coca put the car in drive, heading toward her crib on the north side. Her mind was on kill mode the whole time she was driving.

"I'm good," Coca said.

Bullshit ran through her head. *I gotta make an example outta somebody 'round here.*

Bitches think I'm the one to be fucked with. Damn, I can't believe somebody murdered Eve.

"Shit got real out here in these streets. Just hold on, Coca. It'll be okay. I'm here for you all the way." Baller said.

"Thank you, baby." Coca replied.

Coca pulled up to her house on the north side thirty minutes later and parked in the driveway. She popped the trunk with her remote key.

Baller got out, grabbed the bags, and started walking toward the house.

Coca followed behind.

"You so sweet, baby." Coca said.

"Anything for you, Coca baby." Baller said, sticking his tongue out at her.

"Boy, stop playin' before I make you eat this pussy."

Coca made her way to the black couch, sat down, and started counting her money. She grabbed her phone and dialed Nene.

Nene answered on the second ring.

"Hello." Nene said in a soft tone of voice.

"Hey, baby. I miss you. When can a bitch come over and smash you like a Coke can again?" Coca asked.

"Bitch, please! I missed you too. Coca, a bitch was takin' that dick like a champion." Nene laughed. "Bitch, you got me not even talkin' right at this moment."

"Hoe, quit playin' with me all the damn time. What's really good with you?" Coca asked.

"Not shit at the moment." Nene replied.

Baller got up.

"Coca, let me go lay down in your bedroom, get some rest." Baller said.

Baller started walking.

"Nigga, you act like you ain't got nowhere to go. Everything is ready in the bed 'cause tomorrow we hittin' the mall for a minute or two. Hold up, Nene, bitch!"

Coca kept talkin' to Baller about their plans while he walked toward the bedroom.

"Hello! Hello! Coca, bitch!" Nene yelled through the phone.

"Bitch, I'm back. Bitch, did you take my money and drugs out my house?" Coca's voice turned serious. "You know somebody killed Eve at my crib too. Right now, I'm all about business. You know who did this shit, bitch?" Coca asked, yelling through the phone.

"We can handle this any way you wanna handle it, bitch!" Nene said.

Nene grabbed her handgun off the table and raised it in the air.

Boom! Boom! Boom!

"That's what it's gonna sound like when I spray your ass, bitch, and chop you up like fresh fish meat," Nene said. "I'ma—"

Click.

"This bitch hung up on me. I gotta handle Coca soon." Nene dialed Coca's number again.

After several rings—no answer.

"This bitch got me fucked up for real now." Nene said.

"Baller! Baller!"

Coca screamed out his name.

No answer.

"Well, I guess that nigga left without sayin' anything," Coca said to herself, before walking toward the bedroom where Baller said he'd be.

Coca's mind wasn't workin' right.

Baller jumped out from under the bedsheets.

Coca stood over him, starin' at his handsome face.

Baller had stripped out of all his clothes—

He was laid up in the bed naked.

"Oh my God!" Coca screamed at the top of her lungs. "Baller, that dick is huge."

She got close to the bed, stripping out of her clothes, jumping in. She threw the sheets over both of them.

"Baller, you fine as hell."

Coca felt so good in Baller's arms.

His hand slid down to her ass cheeks.

He kissed her neck—just the way she liked.

"Baller, I love you, nigga."

"I love you, baby. I need this in my life." Baller said.

Coca lowered her head, then looked up into Baller's eyes.

She looked like she was ready to cry for help.

"Why you doin' me like this, Coca? I thought I was all you needed. I thought you loved me?" Baller asked.

Coca's voice cracked, her eyes got watery.

Baller felt some type of way. He held her in his arms, kissed her neck.

"Baller, I do love you . . . but there's so much shit goin' on right now."

Baller kissed Coca's lips and squeezed her ass.

She shook her head from side to side.

"Nigga, this shit ain't cool, Baller. You can't be tellin' me you love me but draggin' me through the mud like a bitch. I been by your side since the projects. Yeah, Eve was my bitch, but I was fuckin' you all the time," Coca said.

"Coca, just stop trippin'," Baller said. He rubbed all over her ass, then kissed her on the lips.

Baller cupped Coca's pussy and slid three fingers into her soaking wet heat while biting and sucking on her neck, leaving big hickeys all over.

That shit drove Coca crazy. She fell deeper into the bed, pulling Baller down on top of her.

"Baby, this ain't cool." Baller said.

"Baller, smell that pussy. Do it smell like strawberries?" Coca asked.

Baller ran his fingers by her long nose, then slid them into her mouth. Coca sucked on them like they were his dick.

Baller pulled his fingers out and slid them back inside her pussy, finger-fucking her before lowering his head and sucking on her big clit.

Every now and then, Baller lifted his head to ask if she loved him, but all Coca did was moan and grind her pussy into his face.

He stood up, got between her legs, and pushed them all the way back by her shoulders.

Her pussy sat out like a ripe orange.

"Tell me you love me, Coca," Baller said. He put his dickhead right at her warm opening.

Coca reached between them, trying to force him in, but Baller pulled back.

He ran the head over her clit, teasing, then pushed it inside—

Just the tip.

Then he pulled back out.

Baller needed to hear those words because he knew Coca still loved him.

"Coca, tell me that, and I'll beat that pussy up like you been missin' and want me to," Baller said.

Baller put the tip back in, stroked in and out three times, then held it there—

Then pulled back out again and laid his dick on her wet, sexy lips.

Coca moaned.

"Yes! Yes! Oh, yes, Daddy!"

"You my queen, and I love you more than anything in this world," Baller said.

"Now, please, fuck me harder and harder, nigga!" Coca begged.

"You makin' me fall in love all over again," Baller said.

Coca blinked, and tears slipped down her cheeks. Baller leaned over and kissed each one. Then he took his large dick and slid it into her hot, wet, warm pussy.

Her walls gripped him immediately.

Yeah, this home right here. I gotta beat this pussy up, Baller thought to himself.

"Yes, Daddy! Faster! Faster! I need this dick in my life!" Coca moaned.

Baller's hips slammed into her again and again. He was tryin' to kill that pussy.

"You feel all this dick in your stomach?" Baller asked.

"Yes, baby! Oh, baby, I'm cummin'! Yes, yes! Ahh, shit!" Coca cried out.

"Damn, baby. You no more good for another round or two. Let's get some rest. We got business to handle tomorrow," Baller said.

"You right. Fuck all that. A bitch tired as fuck right now," Coca said.

She rolled over, ready to knock out.

Baller held her tight as they laid together, resting up for the night.

The next morning Coca and Baller got up early, ready to go hit the streets of Blytheville. Coca made sure the duffle bags was safe in the bedroom closet. They headed out the front door, drivin' toward the mall on the east side.

Twenty minutes later, they pulled up.

Coca got out first, headin' straight to her favorite store— Victoria's Secret.

Baller followed right behind, slammin' the car door.

Coca wanted some sexy underwear, so she made her way inside, grabbin' different bra and panty sets. She went into the dressing room to try them on, wantin' to see what Baller thought.

"Coca, I don't even know why you askin' me if I like what you have on. You know damn well I'ma like it. Make me come in there and fuck you in these white folks' store." Baller said.

Right when Coca changed back into her clothes, she stepped out and walked to the register to pay for her stuff. Baller had to adjust his dick 'cause it got semi-hard instantly.

Coca laughed.

"Boy, you should be ashamed of yourself right now," Coca teased.

"Fuck that. This all me, baby," Baller said.

They walked out the store, headed toward the car.

"You so beautiful," Coca said. She kissed Baller on the lips before tossin' their bags in the car.

Then they drove off.

Chapter 17

Nene was at the house watchin' the NFL preseason game between the Chicago Bears and the Green Bay Packers. Her cell phone started ringin' in the middle of the game. She reached for the table, grabbed her phone, and checked the caller ID.

When she saw John's name on the screen—her co-worker—she answered in a soft tone.

"Hello."

"Hey, Nene. Well, you been on my mind these last few days. It's always a pleasure and an honor to call you, baby. The last time we were together, we had a lot of fun, and I been wonderin'—can we make it happen again?" John asked.

"White boy, please! You need to get your money up first, 'cause this pussy cost. You understand a bitch is all about business. John, you know a bitch ate that dick up like a piece of cheesecake." Nene said.

"You did handle your business. You never thought a white man had a large dick and could handle a thick Black woman with a nice round ass. You was moanin' and screamin' the whole time. To be honest, you got some good-ass pussy. Nene, I always made sure you was straight and took care of all your bills. Don't trip—White Boy is here in your corner." John said.

"John, you funny as fuck right now. I got a lot of shit to handle out here in these streets.

That bitch Coca been callin' me, talkin' shit about somebody takin' her money and drugs from her crib. That bitch got me twisted. John, I got so much drugs and money, it's a shame, but I can't get to the stash spot at this moment. Damn, a bitch trippin'—this phone might be tapped by the feds," Nene said.

"Nene, don't play with me like that. You know I been takin' shit from these drug dealers on the street when I stop 'em in traffic. This how I make my livin' out here. Right now, I got about twenty bricks of cocaine and thirty pounds of weed. Nene, I need to push this shit back on the streets soon. A lot of times, cops don't play by the rules—and Nene, I'm one of 'em. I love money, hoes, and clothes." John said.

"You know a bitch been on the same level out here in these streets. Them bitches on the west side hate me, but this bag of money I got gets heavier and heavier by the pound. Right now, I'm not interested in Coca's games—she not on my level. To be honest, I supply her and probably a lot of these other bitches out here. You know she got that nigga Baller whisperin' in her ear right now. John, bring a bitch five bricks of that cocaine, and I'll give them back when I get my shit from my hiding spot," Nene said.

"Nene, I'ma give you five bricks of this pure cocaine on the strength that you been fuckin' with me on all levels of the game. It won't cost you shit back at the moment."

John smiled after making the comment.

"What—you want some more of this good pussy and fire head?" Nene asked.

"Hell yeah, baby!" John yelled through the phone.

"Bring them five bricks, and we'll talk about the rest. I'ma leave the key under the rug on the front porch. I'ma be in my bedroom layin' down 'cause I got a headache," Nene said.

While she was talkin' to John, she got up, walked outside, and slid the house key under the rug. Then she rushed back inside, went straight to the bedroom, and got undressed. She jumped in the bed to lay down.

"John, I'll talk to you when you get here," Nene said. "Bye."

John headed to the garage to grab the five bricks of cocaine. He grabbed a black duffle bag to put all five bricks inside. He lifted the washing machine up, looked underneath, grabbed the five bricks, and let the washing machine down slowly.

John opened the passenger door to his Range Rover, threw the heavy duffle bag in the backseat, and closed the door. He then opened the driver's door, got inside, and headed out. He hit the garage door button on his keypad to let the garage up. Once he got out of the garage, he let the door back down.

John headed toward Nene's house. His relationship had been rough these last couple of years with his woman. He realized that love waits for no one. His relationship was no longer on good terms. All this shit was going through his mind as he drove to Nene's house.

Damn. Nene was thinking about how she could put a hit on Coca and Baller. She had been working for many drug dealers for almost several years now. Nene was thinking about getting married to someone one day. Her mind was wandering off on many things while she lay in the bed, undercover, butt naked.

Thirty minutes later, John arrived at Nene's house. He got out of the Range Rover, opened the back door, and reached into the backseat, grabbing the duffle bag. He then closed the back door and started walking toward Nene's house with a fast pace. He arrived on the front porch, reached under the black rug, and grabbed the single house key. He unlocked the door and went straight to the bedroom with the duffle bag in his hand.

"Hey baby, you can set the duffle bag on the floor," Nene said with a sexy smile on her face.

"Do you want me to leave?" John asked.

"No, John . . . I don't want you to leave at this moment."

Nene let her truth come out before she let her arms fall, displaying her now erect, pretty breasts. John was lost in thought, unable to say anything at the moment. He leaned in and tenderly kissed her lips. He started getting undressed to jump into the bed with Nene. His dick was hard as a brick of crack. Nene's full, juicy lips felt so soft to him. Once John got into the bed, he saw that Nene was already naked.

They began to kiss more and more. John's long tongue went deep down Nene's throat. He wrapped his arms around her and pulled her closer to his body. Nene pulled away and whispered, "Hold on."

She got up and went into the front room to make sure the door was locked. Her slim waist and petite frame were candy for John's eyes. He watched as her bubble-shaped ass slightly jiggled with each step. Once she made it back, she jumped back into the bed.

John saw the gap between Nene's thighs. He noticed her cleanly shaved love box hanging perfectly. He bit his bottom lip and nodded. Positioning himself in the middle of the bed, he crawled backward like a stripper.

Nene approached and straddled him. She was on fire, ready to fuck at any moment. Her body craved John desperately, and she felt the wetness underneath her.

She was soaked.

She had never wanted a white man so badly. Maybe it was the way he was obsessed with a Black woman—how he talked about Black women.

Maybe it was just the fact that John had crept into her life. Nene couldn't put her finger on it exactly. The only thing she knew was that she wanted him

Not for his money. Not for the material things. Just for him.

"Baby, I love you, Nene," John said.

"I love you too," Nene replied.

She leaned down, and they began to kiss passionately. John gripped her ass cheeks, and she began to grind against him, lightly moaning, wanting so desperately to feel him inside her.

John enthusiastically kissed Nene's neck while massaging her back. At this point, he was rock-hard and ready to show her what he really had, but Nene had plans.

She aggressively pushed him onto his back, then crawled up, lining her pussy directly over his mouth, and suddenly dropped down, putting all her weight on his face.

Nene smashed her soaked, hot pussy onto his mouth, the wetness making a loud slurping noise throughout the room.

John's hands automatically went to her cheeks, and she began to slowly ride his face, resting her hands on the bed. She moved her hips in slow, circular motions like a stripper as John showed off his mouth skills.

John gently sucked Nene's erect clitoris and flicked his tongue from the bottom to the top of it. He smacked her ass, encouraging her to keep going as he noticed her getting more into it with each second that passed.

Nene felt an orgasm coming, and her pace began to pick up. She ground against his mouth vigorously as she approached her peak, losing herself in the pleasure. John couldn't take it anymore and began to pull down a little bit as Nene did her thing on his face.

John got up, grabbed Nene by her waist, and sat her square on his dick, causing her to moan in pain. Nene panted heavily as John's thickness filled her up. That's when she felt the difference that only his curved dick could provide—that curve hit different.

Nene was pleasantly surprised; she had never been with a white man, let alone one whose dick was so huge.

She moaned and quickly put her hand over her mouth as she closed her eyes, feeling them begin to roll to the back of her head. Slowly, she slid all the way down on his dick and began to gently rock back and forth.

John went deeper inside her, making her squirm and moan louder.

Her plump cheeks slammed down on his testicles as they grooved in unison. Both of them played the "quiet game," neither able to let out the moans and nasty talk they desperately wanted to release.

John picked Nene up with authority, wanting to switch positions. She bit her bottom lip as she got on all fours. She buried her face in the bed, tilted her backside up for easier access, and busted it wide open for a package only John could deliver.

He slowly entered her from the back and rested his hands on the small of her back as she began to move in and out.

Nene gripped the bed sheets, experiencing pleasure and hurt simultaneously.

John made love to her, her eyes rolling to the back of her head out of pure bliss.

Nene almost moaned out loud like a pitbull, but she quickly buried her face in the pillow to muffle the sound.

John looked down as he stroked harder, watching as the ripple effect went through her plump cheeks. He was totally engrossed in the woman in front of him.

Nene looked back at him while he stroked her, and her look made him even firmer as he admired her effortless beauty.

Sweat dripped from his face and dropped onto her back, their flesh slapping against each other.

She reached underneath herself and placed three fingers directly on her clitoris. She began to rub in circular motions as John continued to please her. The action heightened her senses, bringing her closer to a climax.

John noticed she was becoming even more soaked as she played with herself. His nuts swung back and forth with each stroke, causing a smacking noise to fill the air. He slowed down, not wanting to make too much noise. He pulled out of Nene and laid on his back.

Like clockwork, Nene turned around and straddled him. She grabbed his dick and guided it inside her wet pussy. She slowly began to gyrate her hips while sliding up and down on him.

They looked into each other's eyes and almost instantly smiled, knowing they had found something special. They had a physical, mental, and spiritual connection that was simply explosive.

They made love until the morning light, whispering under the covers, laughing and enjoying themselves.

John snuck out just before the sun came up.

It was the beginning of a love that would shake both of their lives. Their secret love affair would be one for the history books, characterized by passionate lovemaking.

Chapter 18

Three months later, the radio dispatch was the soundtrack of daily life. There existed a harmony between the two officers, Nene and John. Their love story unfolded amidst the chaos of their demanding careers, where they found solace and understanding in each other's company.

They were partners on duty, each other's unfailing support through endless and perilous situations, allowing a deep affection and respect to blossom between them. Their synchronicity was the subject of admiration among their colleagues; they moved as a single entity during operations, could complete each other's reports with their eyes closed, and shared laughter during those rare quiet moments at the station.

Love, it seemed, was the most cunning of thieves, having stolen their hearts when they least expected it.

However, this smooth cadence faced an unexpected change in rhythm when, on one ordinary day, amidst the autumn leaves that danced around the precinct steps, John knelt down on one knee and held out a small velvet box to Nene. The weight of the moment pressed on his shoulders as he looked up to meet her eyes, expectant and hopeful.

But the words Nene uttered next were not the ones he had longed to hear. She denied his marriage proposal.

The denial carved a deep chain in John's heart, and he felt an anchor drop within him, pulling his mental wellness into a murky abyss. He wrestled with thoughts dark and untamed, where hurt turned into a bitterness that beckoned him toward malice.

The sight of Nene, once a source of joy, became a sharp reminder of his anguish. In his tormented state, he teetered on the edge of acting upon a harmful impulse—one that could sever their bond and taint his soul.

Yet, in a moment of self-clarity, John realized that vengeance would not heal, nor would it regain the affection he yearned for. He wanted to revive the beauty that once defined their relationship, hoping that perhaps Nene's heart might still be swayed.

So, with newfound resolve, he embarked on a mission not of revenge but of redemption and love. He sought out a gesture—grand yet gentle—one that spoke of his true essence. John decided upon a gift: a small, endearing French Bulldog whose eyes sparkled with innocence and whose playful antics could soften even the sternest hearts. He invested a considerable sum, a testament to his commitment and the depth of his feelings. When John presented the little creature to Nene, her eyes brimmed with tears—not of sorrow, but a complex weave of emotions.

The bulldog waddled towards her with earnest clumsiness, and as Nene scooped the tiny thing into her arms, a tear escaped and traced a line down her cheek.

She understood.

This was not a bribe or a token; it was a symbol of unconditional love, of vulnerability, and of John's willingness to continue cherishing her without the promise of a bond sealed by marriage.

Whether this gesture would be enough to rekindle a romantic love in Nene's heart remained unknown, but one thing was certain—it had reminded her of the John she adored.

The passionate, caring man who wanted to do right by those he cherished, even at his lowest point.

This act of pure kindness had sown a seed—one that had the potential to blossom into something profound once again.

But only time could tell.

***

Two years had passed since Karla and Red had made the bold decision to turn their lives around. The violence and chaos that once surrounded them felt like a distant nightmare as the couple stood hand in hand, exchanging vows under the sheltering canopy of an old willow tree.

It was a small, intimate wedding, with the soft strumming of a guitar in the air and the sun setting behind them, painting the sky in shades of purple. Both of them had been attending historically Black colleges. Karla, with a gentle smile, slipped a sparkling diamond ring onto Red's finger—a ring so immaculate and unique, it captured the essence of Red's bold spirit with its fire, a symbol of their enduring love.

In the days following their nuptial bliss, they began the process of adoption, driven by the desire to share their newfound peace with a child in need. Their journey was filled with anticipation and love, culminating in the moment they first met their son, Lucas—a bright-eyed young boy with an infectious giggle and a heart eager for love. Love was what Karla and Red were ready to provide in abundance, as they had promised each other on their wedding day.

Together, they embarked on a new chapter, leaving behind the cacophony of their former lives for the promise of a serene future. The small family found solace in a quaint home, nestled at the edge of a picturesque town, far removed from the violence that once plagued their lives. The move marked a significant change—one that was felt in the way mornings greeted them with birdsong instead of sirens, and neighbors waved hello with genuine smiles. It was in this welcoming embrace of their new community that Karla,

Red, and Lucas planted their roots, nourishing their family bond in the tranquility they had long yearned for.

Karla often spent her evenings sitting on the porch, studying her college material before she had to take her final exam. Red had already completed hers, passed it, and received her degree. Karla also watched Lucas chase fireflies in the garden, his laughter carrying on the wind like a sweet melody. Red would join her, wrapping an arm around Karla and resting her head against her shoulder—a stark contrast to the chaos that once defined their existence. The diamond ring on Red's finger would catch the fading light, flashing with a brilliance that mirrored the life they had built: a life of love, safety, and endless possibility.

As the years unfolded, the past became a fading shadow that scarcely seemed their own. Red often reminisced about the day Karla proposed, with the ring that still sparked conversations with its unique beauty—a physical testament to Karla's dedication and their steep climb from darkness into the warmth of family and home. Their individual spirits had woven into an unbreakable tapestry, each thread reinforcing their commitment to one another and to the vibrant life they cultivated together, away from the world's tumult and turmoil.

Red and Karla's journey through college was fraught with hurdles that jeopardized the very dream they each held dear—earning their degrees. They enrolled at a historically Black college and university (HBCU)—Howard University—determined to thrive in an institution known for empowering Black excellence despite society's systemic barriers. Yet, the gates of Howard did not insulate them from the prickly underbrush of racism and condescending stereotypes from others who doubted their intellect and their academic pursuits, draining their energies in a struggle that seemed endless.

One day, while reading the newspaper, Karla came across an article about Baller and Coca, who had also turned their lives around. According to the article, Coca was now an assistant pastor at a local church, and Baller was a teacher's aide, a mentor to inmates in different prisons, as well as an author who had written several books.

Time had changed all of them, including Nene and John, each of them now on a different journey in life.

Karla sat the newspaper down, thinking about how great life had been. She and Red had waded through murky waters, battling the strong currents of economic disadvantage that tried to sweep their college goals out to sea.

Scholarships and grants were life preservers, but the storm of tuition fees, textbooks, and living expenses relentlessly threatened to sink them at every turn. Karla juggled multiple jobs, trading sleep for shifts at the local diner, her tips often the difference between a full meal or an empty stomach. Red, aware of the tightrope of financial stability, took up late-night work in the university library, her eyes scanning pages of assignments and studies, her hands equally adept at organizing rows of literature while handling her own academic workload. The balance between work and education was a delicate dance—one misstep away from collapse. Yet, they supported each other, a duo bound by common struggles and mutual aspirations, each success and setback shared and shouldered together.

Over the twisting rollercoaster of many years, the triumphs and trials of their college experience wove a story of resilience. The times they were denied opportunities due to the color of their skin and gender only fueled their determination. Many people made fun of them because they were a same-sex couple in love. But as time went on, they became regular faces in study groups, adding their viewpoints to classrooms buzzing with debates and discoveries. Their voices, once hesitant, grew assured— leaders in discussions and advocates in student organizations, carving out space for themselves and others like them.

As they neared the culmination of their collegiate journey, their list of accomplishments was marked by academic honors, community service awards, and the profound respect of their peers and professors. Each day forged another link in the chain of their endurance, and before they knew it, graduation loomed on the horizon—a testament to the relentless struggle of the years gone by. Karla and Red's graduation from college had not been an easy road, but they got the job done.

As the days melted into weeks, the weight of Coca's secret began to tug at the seams of her spirit. Baller, noticing her frequent retreats into silence, tried to reach out. Their conversations, once full of laughter and lighthearted bickering, now touched on deeper, more sensitive themes. Baller spoke of redemption, of the inherent courage in facing one's truth, regardless of public scrutiny. But Coca's responses were evasive, clouded by the internal storm brewing within her heart.

Baller's worry for Coca deepened with each passing day as he observed her wrestling with her private turmoil. The magnetism between Coca and the woman she had grown close to was undeniable, an attraction that didn't fade despite the hushed conversations ignited within the church walls. He watched as Coca's usual confidence was replaced by a solemnity that hung heavily around her shoulders.

Meanwhile, John readied himself for the release of his latest book—an exploration of identity that he hoped would resonate with young readers. His past works had already scratched the surface of the inner battles one faces, but this was to be his opus—a work that would challenge and inspire, capturing the struggle of evolving while belonging.

In the shadows of this unfolding drama, Nene remained vigilant, a sentinel in the night. She, too, had felt the sting of lost love. The memory of John's proposal lay buried beneath her badge—a reminder of decisions made and paths that had diverged. Her attention, though, was captured by rumors of a developing storm within the congregation she had grown to respect. Nene's detective instincts told her that the narrative was incomplete, that layers beneath the surface remained hidden, waiting to emerge.

Remember, all of them had been fucking on each other in the past, and now things had changed over the last few years. Nene's son had become a man of success, and time continued to flow.

On the eve of a solemn congregation meeting—where whispers of Coca's fate would be addressed—Baller stood outside the church door in a short mini skirt with no panties underneath, her heart heavy with mixed emotions. Coca walked in and headed straight to the backroom where church meetings were held. Someone was already waiting there, ready to go over church material and discuss the upcoming field trip to Atlanta.

When she arrived in the backroom, she found Bonnie standing there, dressed like a man with a strap-on and a ball cap on her head. Their eyes met, and they kissed each other fast. Bonnie grabbed the strap-on with her hand, swinging it back and forth against Coca's legs. Then Bonnie reached her middle finger up Coca's dress, sliding it into her pussy, stroking back and forth.

"Ahh shit, this feels good," Coca moaned.

"Turn around and bend over the chair," Bonnie told her in a soft tone.

Coca stood on her tiptoes, turned around, and kissed Bonnie on the lips. Bonnie slid her hands down Coca's back and cuffed her ass cheeks. Coca's cheeks were fluffy like a pillow and hot. She squeezed the strap-on before inserting it inside her pussy.

"Damn, this feels exciting," Coca said.

Boonie inserted more and more of the strap-on into Coca's pussy.

Bam! Bam! Bam!

Boonie pounded harder and faster, refusing to stop until Coca came.

"Damn, Coca, you sexy as fuck," Boonie said.

The air was thick with anticipation when suddenly, the back door swung open. A figure bolted down the church hallway toward the back room where Coca and Boonie were going at it.

It was Deacon Jones. His breaths came in labored gasps, his usual composed face distorted by urgency. Baller, who had been standing near the entrance of the hallway, caught sight of the Deacon's panicked expression. Their eyes met— a silent exchange passing between them—and Baller knew.

Something was wrong.

"Ahh, baby, right there!" Coca screamed out.

"Yes, yes, big daddy! Kill this pussy!" she moaned.

Down the hallway, Deacon Jones came rushing toward Baller, his face twisted with urgency. He grabbed Baller's arm.

"Baller!" the Deacon exclaimed.

Baller turned his head just as the sounds of bare skin slapping filled the air. The moans, the wetness, the intensity—it was all coming from the back room.

"Oh my God," Baller muttered, words catching in his throat. His chest tightened as he broke into a run, screaming like a bitch down the hallway. He couldn't believe what he was hearing.

He skidded to a stop at the doorway and saw it all— Boonie pounding Coca mercilessly with a long strap-on, Coca gripping the chair, lost in pleasure.

Baller's face twisted in rage. Without thinking, he darted into the kitchen, grabbed the first thing he saw—a long knife—and sprinted back down the hallway.

"Hold up!" Deacon Jones' voice boomed. "You cannot kill these women in this church house." His voice was firm, almost commanding.

Baller stood there, trembling, the knife gripped tight in his hand. His chest rose and fell rapidly, his eyes locked on Coca.

"Deacon, please tell that woman to take some of that out of my baby's pussy!" Baller pleaded, his voice cracking. "She punishing Coca in there! All these years, all I done is love Coca and her kids. Now my heart is broken. Sometimes love hurts, but not like this. Deacon Jones, once again, please tell that woman to take some of that out of my girl."

Baller's grip loosened. The weight of the moment crushed him. With a deep, shaky breath, he let the knife slip from his hand. It clattered to the floor.

Without another word, Baller turned and ran out the side door of the church, straight to his car.

When Baller got to his car, he grabbed his cell phone and dialed Coca's number, but she didn't answer.

After all these years, Baller had never caught Coca cheating on him, and this was a hard pill to swallow at this moment.

Baller reached under the driver's seat and grabbed his handgun. He put the gun to his head, his finger on the trigger.

Hell nawl, Baller quickly said to himself.

Baller rolled down the driver's window and threw the loaded handgun into the church grass. He started up his car and drove off the church lot.

Baller's cell phone started ringing, and he answered on the third ring.

"Hello," Baller said.

"Nigga, please! I love you so much. I want you to know that you could've joined the fucking marathon, but you decided to run away. The bitch that was fucking me with the strap-on? Her name is Boonie, and she belongs to this church. Is there any way I can make this up to you, baby?" Coca asked.

"Nawl. I just want you to come home so we can have a short talk about the whole situation. You know I heard you moaning down the church hallway, and Deacon Jones thought something was going wrong in the back room. Come to find out, Coca, you had ten or eleven inches of plastic dick inside your pussy. I'll see you when you make it home."

Click.

"Boonie, fuck that nigga," Coca said.

Coca and Boonie continued to fuck for about thirty more minutes before Coca tapped out and had to leave the church to go home.

Chapter 19

Nene, once the rejected lover of John, found unexpected solace in the success of her former partner's writing career. She often caught herself marveling at his resilience, the way his words uplifted the troubled spirits of young people in their community and beyond. She bought a copy of every book he published—a silent supporter of the path he had carved from his pain. At that moment, she even considered giving John some more pussy to keep him calm.

John, for his part, poured his heartbreak and growth into the pages of his books. His stories of courage and overcoming adversity weren't just fiction; they were fragments of his soul laid bare for the world to see. Reading about social justice warriors like Tony Daniels fueled his literary crusade, pushing him to write more, to say more, to be more.

Meanwhile, the scandal of Bonnie and Coca's affair had begun to fade into the fabric of the church's history. The congregation, shaken at first, slowly settled into a new normal. Grace and forgiveness—so often preached in scripture—became the lived experiences shaping their relationships. The road to acceptance wasn't easy; it was strewn with the debris of past judgments and the rubble of rigid dogmas.

But life, as it always does, moved on. The choir sang just as fervently, the Sunday school children recited their verses with eagerness, and the community outreach program pressed forward. The church became a microcosm of the outside world, reflecting the same struggles and triumphs found beyond its walls.

Just as Coca had her congregation, Bonnie found a community of her own. She took solace in the local arts scene, discovering a passion. But tonight her focus was elsewhere. As she arrived at the church for a meeting the Deacon had set up, fear and determination warred within her. She hesitated for a brief moment at the entrance of the church before pushing through the doors, drawn forward by an instinct she couldn't ignore. Her connection to Coca wasn't just a fleeting romance; it was a bond forged in vulnerability and truth.

She made her way down the dimly lit hall to the Deacon's office, her pulse thrumming in her ears. Taking a steadying breath, she knocked twice, then turned the handle.

Inside, the atmosphere was thick with tension. The Deacon sat behind his desk, his expression calm but unreadable. Baller leaned against the far wall, arms crossed, his jaw tight. The only sound in the room was the faint murmur of the congregation outside.

Bonnie stepped inside and nodded at the Deacon. 'Good evening, sir.'

The Deacon returned her greeting with a slow nod. 'Bonnie.' His voice was measured, though something unreadable flickered in his eyes.

She turned to Baller. "Hey, Baller."

He didn't respond. Didn't even look at her. His gaze remained fixed on a spot on the wall, his silence carrying more weight than words ever could.

Bonnie's stomach clenched, but she refused to let it shake her. She took a seat, folding her hands in her lap. The room smelled of old wood and faint traces of incense, but beneath that, there was something else—unease, thick in the air, pressing against them all.

Coca should have been here by now.

Bonnie glanced between the two men, then at the empty chair beside her. "Where's Coca?"

Silence.

The Deacon exhaled, resting his elbows on his desk. Baller shifted, finally dragging a hand over his face.

Outside, the muffled hum of the congregation seemed to grow louder, pressing in from beyond the office walls. The weight of Coca's absence settled over them, a silent question hanging in the air.

What the hell was going on?

The murmurs outside swelled into a crescendo, the congregation restless with anticipation. Inside the Deacon's office, the silence was suffocating.

Baller shifted, his jaw tightening as he checked his watch. Coca was late—too late. The longer the clock ticked forward, the heavier her absence became.

The Deacon tapped his fingers against the desk, his usual air of patience starting to wear thin. "Has anyone heard from her?" His voice was steady, but there was an edge to it now.

Bonnie swallowed hard. She pulled out her phone, checking her messages again. Nothing. She shook her head. "No. She said she'd be here."

Baller exhaled sharply, running a hand down his face. Something was off. He felt it deep in his gut. Coca wasn't the type to ghost a meeting—especially not one like this.

Then—

The silence grew heavier.

Bonnie shifted in her seat, arms crossed tight over her chest. The Deacon drummed his fingers against the desk, his usual patience wearing thin.

Baller pushed off the wall, pacing toward the window, tension rolling off him in waves.

The night outside felt unnaturally still. Too still. Bonnie stole a glance at the door. Any second now, Coca should be walking in. But she didn't.

The clock on the wall ticked. The weight of the moment pressed in.

Bonnie. Baller. The Deacon

Separate lives, intertwined fates.

All waiting.

Waiting for the next moment to shatter the fragile balance of their world.

***

Nene's son, Karl, drew a sharp breath as the scene unfolded before him in the dim alleyway. The flickering neon glow from a nearby sign cast eerie shadows over Melvin, but what gripped Karl's senses was the stark contrast of crimson against the dull fabric of Melvin's jeans. Blood from a gunshot wound streamed steadily down Melvin's left leg. This was strange because nobody was around at that moment. Karl was thinking about who did this to Melvin. Was this the act of a random drug war about some street shit or was someone out to kill him because of his family.

"Melvin!" Karl called out, his voice choked with rising panic, barely reaching above a whisper.

Melvin's face was ashen, his wide eyes betraying the shock gripping his body. He leaned heavily against the cold brick wall, looking like a marionette cut from its strings, ready to collapse at any moment.

Karl's mind raced. What started as a simple walk to clear his head had nosedived into a waking nightmare. He wasn't a medic—hell, he could barely handle paper cuts without getting squeamish. Blood had never been his ally, and now the sight of it wrapped around him like a suffocating blanket, threatening to pull him under.

Still, he forced himself forward. He barely knew Melvin beyond the occasional nod in the elevator, the polite "good mornings" exchanged in passing. But none of that mattered now.

"What happened, man?" Karl asked, his breath unsteady.

Melvin swallowed hard, his voice a shaky rasp. "Nigga came outta nowhere . . . caught me slippin'."

Karl's stomach clenched. "Who? What you mean?"

Melvin winced as he shifted against the wall. "I was headed to my cousin's crib… some dude popped out the cut, hoodie on, masked up. Thought he was gon' rob me. I ain't even get a chance to react before I felt it—burnin' like fire in my leg."

Karl's eyes dropped to the wound.

"I'm gonna call for help," Karl said, his voice steadier than he felt. He fumbled for his phone, but as the grim reality of the scene sank in, his knees buckled. The world lurched. His vision blurred. The sounds around him dulled to a distant echo. The phone slipped from his grasp as he crumpled to the cold concrete, the ringing in his ears drowning out Melvin's weak cries for help.

Unseen by either man, a shadow stirred at the alley's edge. A bystander had witnessed the entire thing. Moving swiftly from the darkness, she was a presence of quiet authority—an off-duty security officer, dressed in the dark uniform of her job, but never off guard.

"Stay with me," she barked, her voice sharp yet reassuring.

She dropped to her knees beside Melvin, scanning his wound in an instant. With one hand, she pressed down on the source of the bleeding; with the other, she dialed for emergency services.

Minutes stretched into eternity—time always did that in a crisis. The security officer's training kicked in effortlessly. She ripped a strip from the hem of her shirt, tying it tightly around Melvin's leg to slow the bleeding. His teeth chattered, pain and the cold night air warring for control of his battered body. A low groan escaped his lips as the pressure against his wound increased.

Meanwhile, Karl lay motionless, his pallor deepening. The blood that had sent him spiraling now blurred into the backdrop of his hazy vision. He felt detached from it all, floating somewhere between awareness and oblivion.

Then—

Sirens shattered the silence.

Red and blue lights flashed against the alley's walls. The paramedics swept in, moving with the precision of people who had seen disaster a thousand times before. They clamped down on Melvin's wound, their hands and equipment working in unison to stabilize him.

Karl, barely conscious, felt hands on him—shaking his shoulder, voices shouting commands that barely registered. They were assessing him, making sure he hadn't sustained an injury of his own. But all he felt was the firm yet soothing touch of the security officer, anchoring him back from the abyss of his own fear-induced darkness.

Two lives had been touched by misfortune that night. But salvation had come from an unexpected sentinel.

As the ambulance doors slammed shut, whisking Melvin away to life-saving care, Karl found himself still in the presence of the woman who had changed the course of the night. A spark of admiration—maybe even excitement—stirred in his chest.

They exchanged numbers.

"Will you take me home?" Karl asked, offering a lopsided grin. "I need a hot shower. And I'd like to cook you dinner."

A small smile touched her lips. "I'd be glad to."

They walked to her car. As they drove, Karl guided her toward his place. Then, on impulse, he leaned over and kissed her on the cheek.

"You're so sweet," she murmured. "What's your name?"

"Karl," he replied, his voice steady now.

"What's yours?" Karl asked.

"Mary," she laughed.

"That's an excellent name to have, Mary."

They arrived at Karl's house thirty minutes later. Karl stepped out of the car, walked around to the passenger side, and opened Mary's door with a smile.

"Thank you, Karl."

"You're welcome, Mary."

Karl unlocked the front door, and Mary wasted no time sinking into the couch. He hurried to the bedroom, making sure everything was in place. Satisfied that nothing was out of order, he rushed back into the living room.

"You need anything, baby, before I take a shower?" Karl asked.

"Nawl." Mary stretched, kicking off her shoes.

"A'ight, I'm finna hop in the shower real quick," Karl said, heading back to the bedroom to grab fresh clothes.

The hot water blasted as he stepped under the spray, letting the steam relax his muscles. His mind, though, was running wild. He was supposed to meet up with Benz on the west side, have a sit-down, get back in the game. He needed to focus. But then—

The bathroom door clicked shut.

Karl turned, water dripping down his chest, as Mary stepped inside. She had on nothing but a pair of shorts—with nothing underneath. Her shirt clung to her curves, her nipples pressing against the fabric. The scent of strawberries filled the air.

She locked eyes with him, a slow smile playing on her lips as she closed the door behind her.

Karl ran the towel over his body, his gaze roaming over hers hungrily.

"Baby, I need to go handle some business with Benz on the west side," Karl said, voice thick.

"Who is that?" Mary asked.

"You don't know him like that," Karl replied.

"Okay."

She stepped closer. Her fingers wrapped around his dick, her thumb teasing the tip.

160

"That sound good and all," she purred, "but before you go, you finna fuck this pussy. You might as well turn that shower back on and give me twenty minutes of your hardest strokes."

Mary dropped down, stroking him with slow, deliberate movements. Her tongue flicked over the tip before she took him into her mouth, deep-throating him with her eyes closed.

Karl exhaled hard, his head falling back against the tiled wall. His fingers tangled in her hair as he fucked her mouth in slow motion, his groans echoing in the steamy bathroom. Her suction tightened, the wet slurping sounds mixing with her heavy breathing. Karl moaned, low and deep, his muscles tensing.

Mary pulled off him, letting his dick slide from her lips. She dragged it across her red-stained cheeks, licking up and down his length before taking one ball, then the other, into her mouth.

She looked up, eyes blazing.

"You ready to fuck me, nigga?" Mary asked, her voice dripping with hunger. "This pussy ready for you."

She licked the length of him again, rubbing him against her face, waiting for him to give in.

Karl ain't know what it was, but for some reason, he had to taste that wet pussy. He was fiendin' for it in his mouth. He picked her small ass up and sat her on the edge of the bathtub.

Droppin' to his knees, he spread her thick thighs and sniffed her naked box. His nose brushed against her hole as he spread her lips wide. Damn, she smelled so good. Pussy always smelled good to him—especially when it was free.

Mary moaned, pinched her big clit, then jerked before holding her lips apart.

"You can handle me how you like, nigga. I'm down for whatever 'round this bitch." She grabbed her tits through her tee, rolling them in her palms.

Karl had her pussy wide open, licking up and down her groove. She was already oozing. Drippin' for a real one. Everything that spilled out, he slurped and swallowed. His tongue moved in slow revolutions over her clit, sucking it into his mouth like a baby bottle of milk.

Mary bucked her hips, grinding into his face. She was ridin' him like a young tiger in heat. "Oh shit, Karl!" she gasped, her thighs trembling. She rode his face like a Chevy Caprice flying through the hood at full speed.

"Tell me, nigga, this pussy taste good to you? Tell me now, nigga!" Mary screamed through the bathroom.

Karl was drinking her cum, swallowing, licking, sucking—his tongue flicking in and out of her wet heat.

She clawed at his shoulders, her body jerking as pleasure slammed through her. Then, with a growl, she locked her thick thighs around his head.

Her perfect toes curled against his shoulders, and then—

"Oh shit! Fuck! Yes, Daddy!"

Juices gushed out of her, dripping down his chin, his neck, his chest.

Karl was so damn thirsty for her, he started beating his dick in his hand. He wanted to fuck her right now. He could feel her spit still slick on his shaft, that sloppy wetness like a young thot who knew how to please.

Laying her out on the cold bathroom floor, Karl got between her thighs. Without waiting, he pressed the head of his dick against her puffy lips and slid inside . . .

So wet.

So tight.

The heat of her made him pause—but then he felt it.

The barrier.

Karl stiffened. "Mary. I feel that down there, baby. You sure you want me to break that shit? You better tell me before I do it."

He ripped her tee down the middle, smashing her soft breasts together and sucking her nipple, loving the taste.

When he bit down on the left one, she arched like a cat in danger, a deep moan tearing from her throat.

"Break it, Karl. Take my virginity, young nigga. It's yours. I been wanting somebody to break it all my life, but I couldn't find the right person."

She spread her legs wider, trying to pull him in. Her pussy wrapped around his dick, sucking him in, begging for more.

Karl pulled back, cocking all the way back from Chicago to Arkansas, the head of his dick resting against her small hole.

Then—

He slammed forward.

Tearing through her walls, landing deep inside a wet-ass oven.

Her pussy was *so damn tight*, he nearly nutted on the spot.

"Fuck! Fuck! Aww, shit!" Mary screamed, her nails scraping across his back.

Karl pounded that shit.

Long strokes. Deep strokes. Grown-man shit.

Throwing her legs on his shoulders, he went to work, watching her make the sexiest faces he'd ever seen in his life. She bit down on her bottom lip, her light green eyes squinting with pleasure.

Mary wrapped her arms around his neck, breathing hard as fuck like she was running a race. She arched more and more, taking every inch.

"It hurts some, Karl, but fuck me faster. Faster! Beat this pussy like a set of drummers!"

She sucked all over his lips, moaning into his mouth.

Karl beat at her walls, his dick digging deeper and deeper.

Mary got wetter and wetter, her juices sticking to his sack, leaving a string of slickness every time he pulled out.

The louder she got, the more Karl punished that pussy.

Mary arched her back for the third time, her body convulsing as she came hard, screaming into the towels Karl once wore.

Karl slid between her legs and latched onto her clit, sucking it like he was tryna pull her soul through it. His fingers drilled inside her at full pace until she came again, her body trembling, pussy spasming around him.

"Get on your knees, baby. Come on, hurry up. Put that big ass in the air like a plane in the sky. I gotta have this shit from the back. You too damn thick for me not to." Karl growled.

Mary obeyed, arching her back, looking over her shoulder at him. "You finna turn a bitch out. You finna turn me the fuck out." She bit her lip, shaking her head. "I can't handle all this shit, nigga. You doin' too much."

Karl grabbed a handful of her hair, moving it to the side so he could suck on her neck. His dick brushed up against her soaked pussy, sliding between her lips.

"Reach under your body and put this dick back inside you. Hurry up, baby. You wanted this dick bad, right?"

"Unnn." Mary moaned, reaching back. Her small hands wrapped around him. "Damn, it's so heavy." She lined him up and slid him back inside her wet heat. "Fuck, Karl!" she screamed.

Karl gripped her small waist and got to strokin' like it was the last pussy he'd ever have in his life. So wet. So tight. So goddamn warm—like sinking into a pot of melted honey. Her pussy gripped him, sucked him in, clenched around him like it ain't wanna let go. Each time he pulled back, her walls clung to his dick, coating him in slick, dripping heat. Karl groaned deep, feeling that tight, sticky, grip lock around him as he slammed back in.

That big ass bounced against his stomach every single time she crashed back into him. Mary's large titties did the same, swinging wild. She fucked back on him faster and faster, putting that pussy under a spell.

"Fuck me, Karl! Yes. Yes. Aww, I'm cummin'! I'm cummin'! Karl! You my dude now!" Mary screamed.

Their skin met in a steady, *clap, clap, clap.* Karl was beating that pussy like it owed him money. Mary smashed back onto him hard, and that was all she wrote.

Karl pulled his dick out and stroked it fast, his abs tightening. In seconds, thick ropes of cum splashed across her ass in big globs. He kept stroking, his dick jerking in his hand, watching the way her pussy lips stayed wide open, still twitching.

That sight alone sent a second orgasm ripping through him.

Mary turned all the way around and took his dick into her mouth. Karl groaned deep, running his fingers through her hair, kissing all over her forehead.

Twenty minutes later, they were in the shower.

Karl washed Mary's body, and she washed his, their hands roaming. Every few minutes, they stopped, tongue-kissing, breathing heavy, letting the steam swallow them whole.

Then Mary bent over again.

Karl took her raw from the back, her wetness making it too easy to slide in. He smacked that big booty every few strokes, making it bounce.

This time, the pussy felt even better.

Tighter. Wetter.

He couldn't get enough of it.

He fucked her hard—with no mercy.

They wasn't supposed to be doing what they were doing anyway. But since they was, it was his job to punish that pussy to the fullest.

After Karl came for the fifth time, he carried her into the bedroom and laid her out on his king-size bed. Mary wrapped her arms around his neck, exhausted.

Karl laid her back, spread her thighs, and kissed her bald pussy, licking her from slit to clit before stretching out beside her.

Mary moaned, her hand drifting down between her legs, fingers roaming through her cleft.

"You bad, baby." Karl smirked.

"Thank you for getting a bitch pussy right." Mary kissed him deep, slow, her lips lingering on his for a solid two minutes. Then she pulled back and got up to leave.

"Wait, baby." Karl sat up, watching her grab her clothes. "This can't be the last time. We need to figure somethin' out real quick."

Mary's eyes lit up. She climbed onto the bed, got on her knees, and wrapped her arms around his neck.

"I need a good, handsome nigga like you, Karl. Please be safe in the streets."

She hugged him tight, her warmth sinking into his skin.

Karl leaned back, kissed her forehead. "It's all good, baby. I'm in those streets, but for you? I'll make adjustments."

Mary nodded. "Okay. Please be careful out there. I'll holla at you later."

"Thank you." Karl kissed her forehead one last time before she grabbed her things and walked out the front door.

When the door clicked shut, Karl crawled into bed and pulled the covers over himself, his body still buzzing from the night.

Chapter 20

Many years had passed since Eve was killed in Blytheville, Arkansas. Life wasn't getting any better for Coca. Nene had been on the case, but still—no arrest. No justice. Coca was losing her patience, slowly but surely.

To make shit worse, she and Baller were constantly at each other's throats. The arguing, the tension—it was getting old. She was three steps from packing her shit and leaving town. Lately, she had been staying out late, just like Baller used to do her.

"You fucking somebody else?" Baller asked.

Coca played dumb. She knew exactly what he was talking about. Instead of answering, she closed the door behind her, leaned against it, and slid her hands down his pants, yanking them to the floor.

"Hold up." Baller stepped back and stripped the rest of his clothes off, his dick already standing straight up.

He grabbed her, pulled her closer, and ripped her skirt off, tossing it aside.

Coca was naked now—not that it mattered. She barely wore shit around him anyway.

Baller grabbed her by the legs and dragged her to the edge of the bed. The sudden movement startled her.

"What the fuck you doing, Baller?" Coca asked, breath hitching.

He didn't answer.

Instead, he dove between her legs, spreading her wide.

The warmth of his long tongue melted her instantly.

"Ahh, shit!" Coca screamed, running her fingers through his hair, her thick thighs trembling.

Baller was a young nigga, but he knew exactly what to do to a female body. He sucked on her big clit, flicking his tongue over it before plunging three thick fingers inside her.

"Yes! Yes! Yes!" Coca spread her legs wider, giving him full access to his favorite spot.

He pressed his big thumb against her clit, rubbing it in slow, deep circles.

"Oh shit! Right there, nigga! Don't stop!" Coca screamed.

"You like how I eat that pussy, don't you?" Baller growled against her slick heat.

"Yes, Daddy."

Baller lifted his head, wiped his mouth, then lined himself up and drove inside her, raw and deep.

One of her legs rested on his shoulder, the other wrapped around his waist. He locked in, hitting every single wall. Every stroke had his dick buried to the hilt, slamming inside her warmth. Powerful. Merciless. Punishing.

"Damn, this pussy good. Fuck." Baller groaned.

Coca screamed. "Oh, shit! Fuck me, Daddy! Yes!"

She was too loud.

Baller shoved his fingers into her mouth, muffling her moans before the neighbors heard. He didn't slow down. If anything, that shit made him fuck her harder.

His mind was on fire—thinking about how Coca had cheated on him. Not even with a nigga, but with another bitch. That shit had him mad as fuck. He gripped her hips tight and pounded into her, drilling her insides with mad aggression . . .

Hard. Rough. Deep.

Coca moaned louder, her body thrashing beneath him. He clamped a big hand over her mouth, shutting her up.

"Bitch, you belong to me." Baller growled, his voice low and deadly.

"Yes, baby." Coca gasped, tears slipping down her face. Tears for Baller. Tears for Bonnie. Tears for herself.

"I'm sorry, Baller. I didn't mean for it to happen like that. It was an accident."

Baller let out a deep, broken sob, covering his face with his hands.

Coca's heart clenched. She had never seen him like this.

She sat up and wrapped her arms around him, rocking him back and forth.

She felt his pain.

She felt everything.

But at the same time—her heart still went out to Bonnie.

Shit had happened too fast. Too messy. Too out of control.

Maybe that's why she had disappeared earlier that night. She just couldn't face them—not Baller, not Bonnie, not the Deacon.

She had switched off her phone and laid under the sheets in the dark, trying to shut the world out. Hoping the weight of it all would disappear if she just stayed still long enough.

Or maybe she should've run farther. The thought had crossed her mind—to just driving away, maybe pull over in some secluded spot in the woods, somewhere nobody could find her.

But she didn't.

Instead, she ended up right back here—wrapped up in Baller's arms, both of them drowning in shit neither of them knew how to fix.

They held each other in the dark, emotions raw and tangled, until sleep finally took them both.

Baller sprawled out in the middle of the bed, knocked the fuck out. Exhausted. Not just from the sex—but from the weight of everything. He was fed up with Coca cheating on him with another bitch.

Coca lay beside him, staring at the ceiling.

Her body was drained.

But her mind?

Still at war.

Coca's pussy was sore as hell from the pounding she took from Baller's dick.

Still throbbing. Still stretched.

She lay there, watching him sleep, admiring how fine he looked knocked out cold.

The love she had for Baller was real. Deep. Unshakable.

No one else came close to her heart, but Bonnie.

There were a lot of unanswered questions when it came to Coca—especially after what happened in the back of the church:

Coca was caught in the backroom. Bent over. Getting her pussy drilled by Bonnie with a long pink strap-on dildo to the point Coca was screaming out in pain. Bonnie had her fucked up—literally.

Now, lying next to Baller, she couldn't erase that moment from her mind.

Twenty minutes later, exhausted and drained, she fell asleep in Baller's arms.

Baller woke up out of nowhere, a question burning in his mind. He reached over, gripping Coca's body with both hands.

"What happened back there in the church, Coca? I wanna hear every single detail again." His voice was low but demanding.

Coca blinked, half-asleep. "Hold up, baby." She let out a soft laugh, confused.

Baller wasn't laughing.

"Coca, I don't like that you got another bitch in your life. And you ain't even invite me?" His grip on her waist tightened.

Coca smirked like a shy schoolgirl. She loved testing him.

"Well, the bitch had a long-ass strap-on. Big as fuck."

She ran her fingers through her hair, stretching like she wasn't about to say some wild shit.

"I met Bonnie on Facebook Dating. She had me in so many crazy-ass positions, I literally felt like a pretzel. Bonnie fucked me on the chairs, the table, the floor, the wall—then she picked my ass up and walked around while I bounced on that strap-on like a stripper dancing center-stage in the club."

Baller shook his head, smirking. "You a nasty, freaky-ass bitch. So what—you tryna say my dick ain't gettin' the job done?"

Coca slid her tongue across her lips. "Nah, baby. You know you can. I just wanted to try something different."

She was lying her ass off.

She had been fucking with women for a minute now.

And this was more than just "trying something different."

Coca felt the guilt creeping in. Her chest tightened. Tears welled up in her eyes. She reached for her clothes, pulling them on fast.

"Baby, what you doin'?" Baller asked, sitting up.

She didn't answer.

He jumped up, grabbing her arm, watching her put on her clothes like she was ready to be out.

"I'm cool. Let's go. I got shit to handle." Coca said, brushing past him.

Baller exhaled hard. Something about this felt off.

Still, he didn't press it.

"A'ight." He pulled his clothes on and followed her out the door.

As they got to the car, Baller leaned against the passenger door. "Drop me off at my trap. I'll catch up with you later," Baller said.

Coca nodded, unlocking the doors. "A'ight. That's cool."

She slid behind the wheel, but her mind was racing.

What the fuck was she doing?

***

Bonnie woke up naked in her bed. Her head throbbed, her body felt sore, and the first thing she wondered was—who the fuck moved her from the couch? She rubbed her temples, trying to remember. The local club. The drinks. The bar. But her memory was foggy as hell.

Shaking it off, she stumbled to the bathroom, relieved herself, then stepped into the hot shower.

Damn, she loved this feeling.

The hot water pounded against her thick body, rolling over her curves, relaxing her muscles. Mornings like this were the best—no distractions, no bullshit.

Bonnie closed her eyes, letting the heat wash over her.

Then—the pressure from the showerhead slipped between her legs.

Her body reacted before her mind could catch up.

Fuck. I haven't had sex since Coca, she thought.

She tried to think back—who was the last person that really tamed this pussy? Who had stroked her to the point of multiple orgasms, had her screaming, dripping, shaking?

Then, out of all people—Deacon Jones popped up in her head.

Bonnie smirked to herself.

Slowly, she eased her right hand between her thighs, her fingers slipping into the heat of her wet pussy.

She imagined Deacon Jones gripping her hips, throwing her leg over his shoulder, fucking her against the wall like he owned her.

"Oh shit, Deacon Jones!" she moaned out loud, her voice breathless, needy.

She wanted to scream louder, but the only sounds that came out were erotic moans of pleasure.

In her mind, he was deep inside her—

Stroking.Pounding.Thrusting his thick dick in and out, teasing her clit, hitting her hot spot every single time.

"A couple more strokes, baby . . . I'm almost there," Bonnie gasped, her breath coming in sharp bursts.

The sensation built deep inside her—hot, intense, ready to explode like a weapon of mass destruction.

She knew this one was gonna be powerful.

So, like the beast she was, she braced herself for the tidal wave about to take her under.

Her body tightened, her breathing hitched, her thighs trembled—

Then—

BAM!

"Excuse me, baby, but I gotta use the bathroom real bad!"

The door swung open.

Bonnie jumped back against the tub, eyes flying open, heart slamming against her chest.

"What the fuck!"

She scrambled to cover herself, still dripping, still throbbing, still seconds away from the orgasm that was just ripped from her.

TO BE CONTINUED

Lock Down Publications and Ca$h Presents
Assisted Publishing Packages

Due to an increase in the price of services we have increased our prices. The prices below reflect the price increase as of 11/1/24.

BASIC PACKAGE	UPGRADED PACKAGE
$699	**$1000**
Editing	Typing
Cover Design	Editing
Formatting	Cover Design
	Formatting
	Upload eBooks to Amazon
	Upload Paperback to Amazon
ADVANCE PACKAGE	**LDP SUPREME PACKAGE**
$1,400	**$1,700**
Typing	Typing
Editing (line editing/content)	Editing (line editing/content)
Cover Design	Cover Design
Formatting	Formatting
Copyright Registration	Copyright Registration
Proofreading	Proofreading
Upload eBooks to Amazon	Set up Amazon Account
Upload Paperback to Amazon	Upload eBooks to Amazon
	Upload Paperback to Amazon
	Advertise on LDP's Amazon and Facebook Page

***

Other services available upon request.
Additional charges may apply

Lock Down Publications
P.O. Box 944
Stockbridge, GA 30281-9998
Phone: 470 303-9761
Email: lockdownpublications@gmail.com

Submission Guideline

Submit the first three chapters of your completed manuscript to ldpsubmissions@gmail.com. In the subject line add **Your Book's Title**. The manuscript must be in a Word Doc file and sent as an attachment. Document should be in Times New Roman, double spaced, and in size 12 font. Also, provide your synopsis and full contact information. If sending multiple submissions, they must each be in a separate email.

Have a story but no way to send it electronically? You can still submit to LDP/Ca$h Presents. Send in the first three chapters, written or typed, of your completed manuscript to:

LDP: Submissions Dept
P.O. Box 944
Stockbridge, GA 30281-9998

DO NOT send original manuscript. Must be a duplicate. Provide your synopsis and a cover letter containing your full contact information.

Thanks for considering LDP and Ca$h Presents.

NEW RELEASES

BLOODLINE OF A SAVAGE 1-3
THESE VICIOUS STREETS 1-3
RELENTLESS GOON 1-3
BY PRINCE A. TAUHID

THE BUTTERFLY MAFIA 1-3
BY FUMIYA PAYNE

A THUG'S STREET PRINCESS 1&2
BY MEESHA

CITY OF SMOKE 3
BY MOLOTTI

GET IT IN SLUGS 1 &2
BY B. STALL

STANDING ON HER BUSINESS 1&2
BY DG SANTANA

STEPPERS 1,2&3
THE REAL BADDIES OF CHI-RAQ
BY KING RIO

THE LANE 1&2
BY KEN-KEN SPENCE

THUG OF SPADES 1&2
LOVE IN THE TRENCHES 2
CORNER BOYS
BY COREY ROBINSON

TIL DEATH 3
BY ARYANNA

THE BIRTH OF A GANGSTER 4
BY DELMONT PLAYER

PRODUCT OF THE STREETS 1-3
BY DEMOND "MONEY" ANDERSON

NO TIME FOR ERROR
BY KEESE

MONEY HUNGRY DEMONS 1-2
BY TRANAY ADAMS

HUB CITY MENACE 1-3
BY J. WHITE

A THUGGISH PASSION 1&2
LAND OF DA HOOLIGANZ 1-4
KILLAZ ON STANDBY 1&2
BY IRA B.

FO'EVA ROLLIN 1&2
BY ASSA RAYMOND BAKER

THE LEVEL UP 1&3
BY LUXURY KING

Coming Soon from Lock Down Publications/Ca$h Presents

IF YOU CROSS ME ONCE 6
ANGEL V
By Anthony Fields

A THUGS STREET PRINCESS 3
By Meesha

CORNER BOYS 2
By Corey Robinson

THA TAKEOVER
By Keith Chandler

BETRAYAL OF A G 2
By Ray Vinci

SAVAGE FAMILY EMPIRE 1&2
SOULLESS GOON 1,2&3
THE DIRTY SIDE OF MONEY 1,2&3
By Prince

FOR MY ENEMY'S SAKE
AMBITIONS OF A SLIDER
FRESH OFF DA PORCH
By IRA B.

THE TRUCKLOAD 1-4
TIPPIN' THE SCALES 1-3
BAD BITCHES WIT GUNZ 3
PROBLEM SOLVED 2
By Christopher "Diesel" Hornezes

Available Now

RESTRAINING ORDER 1 & 2
By **CA$H & Coffee**

LOVE KNOWS NO BOUNDARIES 1-3
By **Coffee**

RAISED AS A GOON I, II, III & IV
BRED BY THE SLUMS I, II, III
BLAST FOR ME I & II
ROTTEN TO THE CORE I II III
A BRONX TALE I, II, III
DUFFLE BAG CARTEL I II III IV V VI
HEARTLESS GOON I II III IV V
A SAVAGE DOPEBOY I II
DRUG LORDS I II III
CUTTHROAT MAFIA I II
KING OF THE TRENCHES
By **Ghost**

LAY IT DOWN I & II
LAST OF A DYING BREED I II
BLOOD STAINS OF A SHOTTA I & II III
By **Jamaica**

LOYAL TO THE GAME I II III
LIFE OF SIN I, II III
By **TJ & Jelissa**

IF LOVING HIM IS WRONG…I & II
LOVE ME EVEN WHEN IT HURTS I II III
By **Jelissa**

PUSH IT TO THE LIMIT
By **Bre' Hayes**

BLOODY COMMAS I & II
SKI MASK CARTEL I, II & III
KING OF NEW YORK I II, III IV V
RISE TO POWER I II III
COKE KINGS I II III IV V
BORN HEARTLESS I II III IV
KING OF THE TRAP I II
By **T.J. Edwards**

WHEN THE STREETS CLAP BACK I & II III
THE HEART OF A SAVAGE I II III IV
MONEY MAFIA I II
LOYAL TO THE SOIL I II III
By **Jibril Williams**

A DISTINGUISHED THUG STOLE MY HEART I II & III
LOVE SHOULDN'T HURT I II III IV
RENEGADE BOYS 1-4
PAID IN KARMA 1-3
SAVAGE STORMS 1-3
AN UNFORESEEN LOVE 1-3
BABY, I'M WINTERTIME COLD 1-3
A THUG'S STREET PRINCESS 1&2
By **Meesha**

A GANGSTER'S CODE 1-3
A GANGSTER'S SYN 1-3
THE SAVAGE LIFE 1-3
CHAINED TO THE STREETS 1-3
BLOOD ON THE MONEY 1-3
A GANGSTA'S PAIN 1-3
BEAUTIFUL LIES AND UGLY TRUTHS
CHURCH IN THESE STREETS
By **J-Blunt**

CUM FOR ME 1-8
An LDP Erotica Collaboration

REDEMPTION IN THE STREETS | TONY DANIELS

BLOOD OF A BOSS 1-5
SHADOWS OF THE GAME
TRAP BASTARD
By **Askari**

THE STREETS BLEED MURDER 1-3
THE HEART OF A GANGSTA 1-3
By **Jerry Jackson**

WHEN A GOOD GIRL GOES BAD
By **Adrienne**

THE COST OF LOYALTY 1-3
By **Kweli**

BRIDE OF A HUSTLA 1-3
THE FETTI GIRLS 1-3
CORRUPTED BY A GANGSTA 1-4
BLINDED BY HIS LOVE
THE PRICE YOU PAY FOR LOVE 1-3
DOPE GIRL MAGIC 1-3
By **Destiny Skai**

A KINGPIN'S AMBITION
A KINGPIN'S AMBITION II
I MURDER FOR THE DOUGH
By **Ambitious**

TRUE SAVAGE 1-7
DOPE BOY MAGIC 1-3
MIDNIGHT CARTEL 1-3
CITY OF KINGZ 1&2
NIGHTMARE ON SILENT AVE
THE PLUG OF LIL MEXICO 1&2
CLASSIC CITY
By **Chris Green**

A GANGSTER'S REVENGE 1-4
THE BOSS MAN'S DAUGHTERS 1-5
A SAVAGE LOVE 1&2
BAE BELONGS TO ME 1&2
A HUSTLER'S DECEIT 1-3
WHAT BAD BITCHES DO 1-3
SOUL OF A MONSTER 1-3
KILL ZONE
A DOPE BOY'S QUEEN 1-3
TIL DEATH 1-3
IMMA DIE BOUT MINE 1-6
DYING FOR LIKES
By **Aryanna**

A DOPEBOY'S PRAYER
By **Eddie "Wolf" Lee**

THE KING CARTEL 1-3
By **Frank Gresham**

THESE NIGGAS AIN'T LOYAL 1-3
By **Nikki Tee**

GANGSTA SHYT 1-3
By **CATO**

THE ULTIMATE BETRAYAL
By **Phoenix**

BOSS'N UP 1-3
By **Royal Nicole**

I LOVE YOU TO DEATH
By **Destiny J**

I RIDE FOR MY HITTA
I STILL RIDE FOR MY HITTA
By **Misty Holt**

LOVE & CHASIN' PAPER
By **Qay Crockett**

TO DIE IN VAIN
SINS OF A HUSTLA
By **ASAD**

BROOKLYN HUSTLAZ
By **Boogsy Morina**

BROOKLYN ON LOCK 1 & 2
By **Sonovia**

GANGSTA CITY
By **Teddy Duke**

A DRUG KING AND HIS DIAMOND 1-3
A DOPEMAN'S RICHES
HER MAN, MINE'S TOO 1&2
CASH MONEY HO'S
THE WIFEY I USED TO BE 1&2
PRETTY GIRLS DO NASTY THINGS
By **Nicole Goosby**

LIPSTICK KILLAH 1-3
CRIME OF PASSION 1-3
FRIEND OR FOE 1-3
By **Mimi**

TRAPHOUSE KING 1-3
KINGPIN KILLAZ 1-3
STREET KINGS 1&2
PAID IN BLOOD 1&2
CARTEL KILLAZ 1-3
DOPE GODS 1&2
By **Hood Rich**

THE STREETS ARE CALLING
By **Duquie Wilson**

STEADY MOBBN' 1-3
THE STREETS STAINED MY SOUL 1-3
By **Marcellus Allen**

WHO SHOT YA 1-3
SON OF A DOPE FIEND 1-4
HEAVEN GOT A GHETTO 1&2
SKI MASK MONEY 1&2
By **Renta**

GORILLAZ IN THE BAY 1-4
TEARS OF A GANGSTA 1/&2
3X KRAZY 1&2
STRAIGHT BEAST MODE 1&2
By **DE'KARI**

TRIGGADALE 1-3
MURDA WAS THE CASE 1-3
By **Elijah R. Freeman**

SLAUGHTER GANG 1-3
RUTHLESS HEART 1-3
By **Willie Slaughter**

GOD BLESS THE TRAPPERS 1-3
THESE SCANDALOUS STREETS 1-3
FEAR MY GANGSTA 1-5
THESE STREETS DON'T LOVE NOBODY 1-2
BURY ME A G 1-5
A GANGSTA'S EMPIRE 1-4
THE DOPEMAN'S BODYGAURD 1&2
THE REALEST KILLAZ 1-3
THE LAST OF THE OGS 1-3
By **Tranay Adams**

MARRIED TO A BOSS 1-3
By **Destiny Skai & Chris Green**

KINGZ OF THE GAME 1-7
CRIME BOSS 1-4
By **Playa Ray**

FUK SHYT
By **Blakk Diamond**

DON'T F#CK WITH MY HEART 1&2
By **Linnea**

ADDICTED TO THE DRAMA 1-3
IN THE ARM OF HIS BOSS
By **Jamila**

LOYALTY AIN'T PROMISED 1&2
By **Keith Williams**

YAYO 1-4
A SHOOTER'S AMBITION 1&2
BRED IN THE GAME
By **S. Allen**

TRAP GOD 1-3
RICH $AVAGE 1-3
MONEY IN THE GRAVE 1-3
CARTEL MONEY 1&2
By **Martell Troublesome Bolden**

FOREVER GANGSTA 1&2
GLOCKS ON SATIN SHEETS 1&2
By **Adrian Dulan**

TOE TAGZ 1-4
LEVELS TO THIS SHYT 1&2
IT'S JUST ME AND YOU
By **Ah'Million**

KINGPIN DREAMS 1-3
RAN OFF ON DA PLUG
By **Paper Boi Rari**

THE STREETS MADE ME 1-3
By **Larry D. Wright**

CONFESSIONS OF A GANGSTA 1-4
CONFESSIONS OF A JACKBOY 1-3
CONFESSIONS OF A HITMAN
CONFESSIONS OF A DOPE BOY
By **Nicholas Lock**

I'M NOTHING WITHOUT HIS LOVE
SINS OF A THUG
TO THE THUG I LOVED BEFORE
A GANGSTA SAVED XMAS
IN A HUSTLER I TRUST
By **Monet Dragun**

QUIET MONEY 1-3
THUG LIFE 1-3
EXTENDED CLIP 1&2
A GANGSTA'S PARADISE
By **Trai'Quan**

CAUGHT UP IN THE LIFE 1-3
THE STREETS NEVER LET GO 1-3
By **Robert Baptiste**

NEW TO THE GAME 1-3
MONEY, MURDER & MEMORIES 1-3
By **Malik D. Rice**

CREAM 2-3
THE STREETS WILL TALK
By **Yolanda Moore**

THE STREETS WILL NEVER CLOSE 1-3
By **K'ajji**

LIFE OF A SAVAGE 1-4
A GANGSTA'S QUR'AN 1-4
MURDA SEASON 1-3
GANGLAND CARTEL 1-3
CHI'RAQ GANGSTAS 1-4
KILLERS ON ELM STREET 1-3
JACK BOYZ N DA BRONX 1-3
A DOPEBOY'S DREAM 1-3
JACK BOYS VS DOPE BOYS 1-3
COKE GIRLZ
COKE BOYS
SOSA GANG 1&2
BRONX SAVAGES
BODYMORE KINGPINS
BLOOD OF A GOON
By **Romell Tukes**

CONCRETE KILLA 1-3
VICIOUS LOYALTY 1-3
BLOODY MONEY BAGS
By **Kingpen**

THE ULTIMATE SACRIFICE 1-6
KHADIFI
IF YOU CROSS ME ONCE 1-3
ANGEL 1-4
IN THE BLINK OF AN EYE
By **Anthony Fields**

THE LIFE OF A HOOD STAR
By **Ca$h & Rashia Wilson**

NIGHTMARES OF A HUSTLA 1-3
BLOOD AND GAMES 1&2
By **King Dream**

GHOST MOB
By **Stilloan Robinson**

HARD AND RUTHLESS 1&2
MOB TOWN 251
THE BILLIONAIRE BENTLEYS 1-3
REAL G'S MOVE IN SILENCE
By **Von Diesel**

MOB TIES 1-7
SOUL OF A HUSTLER, HEART OF A KILLER 1-3
GORILLAZ IN THE TRENCHES
OOPS CRY TOO 1&2
THE DAUGHTER OF A CARTEL BOSS
By **SayNoMore**

BODYMORE MURDERLAND 1-3
THE BIRTH OF A GANGSTER 1-4
By **Delmont Player**

FOR THE LOVE OF A BOSS 1&2
By **C. D. Blue**

KILLA KOUNTY 1-5
TENDER
By **Khufu**

MOBBED UP 1-4
THE BRICK MAN 1-5
THE COCAINE PRINCESS 1-10
STEPPERS 1-3
SUPER GREMLIN 1-4
A GANGSTA'S SON
By **King Rio**

MONEY GAME 1&2
By **Smoove Dolla**

A GANGSTA'S KARMA 1-5
By **FLAME**

KING OF THE TRENCHES 1-3
By **GHOST & TRANAY ADAMS**

BAD BITCHES WIT GUNZ 1&2
PROBLEM SOLVED
By **"Christopher Diesel" Hornezes**

QUEEN OF THE ZOO 1&2
By **Black Migo**

GRIMEY WAYS 1-3
BETRAYAL OF A G
By **Ray Vinci**

XMAS WITH AN ATL SHOOTER
By **Ca$h & Destiny Skai**

KING KILLA 1&2
By **Vincent "Vitto" Holloway**

BETRAYAL OF A THUG 1&2
By **Fre$h**

COUNTDOWN OF A KILLA 1&2
SEX, MURDER AND GOD 1&2
GUNS DOWN, BOTTOMS UP 1&2
By Lo-Life

THE MURDER QUEENS 1-7
By **Michael Gallon**

FOR THE LOVE OF BLOOD 1-4
By **Jamel Mitchell**

REDEMPTION IN THE STREETS | TONY DANIELS

HOOD CONSIGLIERE 1&2
NO TIME FOR ERROR
By **Keese**

PROTÉGÉ OF A LEGEND 1,2&3
LOVE IN THE TRENCHES 1&2
By **Corey Robinson**

THE PLUG'S RUTHLESS DAUGHTER 1&2
By **Tony Daniels**

BORN IN THE GRAVE 1-3
CRIME PAYS
By **Self Made Tay**

MOAN IN MY MOUTH
By **XTASY**

TORN BETWEEN A GANGSTER AND A GENTLEMAN
By **J-BLUNT & Miss Kim**

LOYALTY IS EVERYTHING 1-3
CITY OF SMOKE 1-3
By **Molotti**

HERE TODAY GONE TOMORROW 1&2
By **Fly Rock**

WOMEN LIE MEN LIE 1-4
FIFTY SHADES OF SNOW 1-3
STACK BEFORE YOU SPLURGE
GIRLS FALL LIKE DOMINOES
NAÏVE TO THE STREETS
By **ROY MILLIGAN**

PILLOW PRINCESS
By **S. Hawkins**

REDEMPTION IN THE STREETS | TONY DANIELS

THE BUTTERFLY MAFIA 1-3
SALUTE MY SAVAGERY 1&2
By **Fumiya Payne**

THE LANE 1&2
By Ken-Ken Spence

THE PUSSY TRAP 1-5
By **Nene Capri**

DIRTY DNA
By **Blaque**

SANCTIFIED AND HORNY
by **XTASY**

BOOKS BY LDP'S CEO, CA$H

TRUST IN NO MAN
TRUST IN NO MAN 2
TRUST IN NO MAN 3
BONDED BY BLOOD
SHORTY GOT A THUG
THUGS CRY
THUGS CRY 2
THUGS CRY 3
TRUST NO BITCH
TRUST NO BITCH 2
TRUST NO BITCH 3
TIL MY CASKET DROPS
RESTRAINING ORDER
RESTRAINING ORDER 2
IN LOVE WITH A CONVICT
LIFE OF A HOOD STAR
XMAS WITH AN ATL SHOOTER

www.ingramcontent.com/pod-product-compliance
Lightning Source LLC
Chambersburg PA
CBHW071208260626
47162CB00004B/1223